When It's All Said and Done

Latifah Ponder

Atlanta, GA

When It's All Said and Done

ISBN: 978-1-7368483-0-2 (print)
ISBN: 978-1-7368483-1-9 (ebook)

Library of Congress Control Number: 2021935614

Printed in the United States of America

Edited by Allwrite Communications

Cover Design by Erin Pritchard

Contents

Author's Note

My name is Latifah Ponder. My dad named me after the queen herself, Queen Latifah. "Queenlala" was a nickname that I came up with as I got older, and many people call me that. You can just call me "Latifah" or "Queenlala" for short as you get to know me and my writings.

I am from a small town, Greenville, Ga., where I attended school until my junior year. I then moved to Senoia, Ga., where I graduated from East Coweta High School. I started writing in middle school. I would often compose short poems, which eventually blossomed into great, fictional stories. I am a very talkative person, so I developed a passion for writing as it gave me the chance to reach my target audiences without coming off as too chatty.

While this book is not dedicated to anyone in particular, it is a way for me to show my greatest appreciation to my biggest supporters: my husband, Ferrando Clark, my dad and my mom, Danny and Nellie Ponder, my best friends in the whole world, my three sisters, Kianna Ponder, Diaundra Ponder, Danyelle Ponder. Thank you all so much for believing in me and being there when I needed you the most. To Danyelle and Ferrando, thank you both for always listening to my new ideas.

I love to write because doing it eases my mind and sends me to a fairytale land where I can be myself without the judgement of others.

I hope you all continue to follow me on my journey with writing. Thank you for the all of your support.

CHAPTER ONE

Laylani

"How you doing, Miss Lady?" asked a guy who approached me from behind.

My best friend, Lea, and I were standing in line for tickets to Gucci Mane's concert. I turned around, and my eyes lit up like a kid on Christmas morning when I saw him. He was standing there looking like God had handmade him and placed him in my presence. His abs poked out of his fitted black V-neck T-shirt. He stood at 6'4" with smooth dark brown skin and perfect white teeth, yielding a perfect smile. Just standing in his presence had my juices flowing. Clearing his throat caused me to come back from space.

"She's fine," Lea said for me. "Her name is Laylani."

My words would not come out. They just seemed to be stuck in my throat.

"Nice to meet you, Laylani. I'm Kingston, but you can call me King." He extended his hand out for me to grab it, but Lea beat me to it. He couldn't do anything but laugh. "Are y'all going to the concert alone?"

"Yes, just me and her," Lea spoke up.

"Lea," I said with a whisper. "I didn't want him knowing that we were going alone." Hell, I didn't even know the guy.

"Girl, loosen up. He's just asking."

He laughed, "I'm sorry. I just couldn't help myself. You're gorgeous."

I mean, I am gorgeous, at least that's what most people tell me. My dad's Black. He is from here in Atlanta, Georgia, where he was born and raised; and my mom is Asian. She is from Mumbai, India. She and her mother moved to America after her husband, my maternal grandfather, died in military service around 1986. My mom was a teenager and attended school here in Atlanta, and that's where she and my dad met. Right before she graduated, my grandma died, so I never met her.

At 5'4", my hair fell to the top of my ass. You would think that I was wearing Brazilian weave, but it was all me baby. People often said that I favored the singer Aaliyah. My ass was just right for my size. My breast were size B cup and my stomach was flat and smooth. My tan was to die for.

"Thanks," I had finally worked up the guts to say. I lowered my head in a bashful shyness and King lifted it up with his finger.

"Don't ever hold your head down in my presence."

I blushed and smiled.

"Give me your phone," he said confidently as he held his hand out. "I'll lock my number in. Call me."

I gave him my phone and he keyed his number in and handed it back to me. We grabbed our tickets and left. He and his friends were still in line.

Lea was laughing the whole walk to the car. "Girl, you looked like a deer in headlights."

"Shut the hell up," I smirked.

Lea was my girl. We had been friends since high school, so she knew me well enough to know what was on my mind.

"I'm just saying. That man had you mesmerized," she said.

I just simply rolled my eyes, and we both got in the car to head back to our apartment.

Lea and I had been roommates since we both moved out of our parents' houses when we were 18. That was four years ago. We're both 22 now.

Once we got home, I went straight to my closet to find the perfect outfit for the night. I decided that I would wear my red, short, fitted dress; it hugged my hips like a glove. My feet were in my red bottoms that I loved to wear. Lea curled my hair for me and applied my makeup. She wore a short white romper that exposed her back, and on her feet, she wore white heels that tied around her calves.

"I'm getting drunk tonight," Lea said, dancing to Gucci Mane's song 'Wasted' that was playing on the radio. I just shook my head at her and laughed. Lea was the more outgoing one of the two of us. I was shy and laid back. Lea and I were the same height, but she had a dark complexion with a pretty baby face. Her ass was round and thick, and she had a slim waist with silky, smooth skin. She was in the mirror shaking her ass. "I'm gon' find me a man tonight, boo."

"What happened to ol' boy?" I asked. She was in a different relationship every damn three months.

"Girl, he broke." She fanned me off.

Lea loved money and even more, she loved *men* with money. I wouldn't say that she was a prostitute, but if you weren't coughing up money before having sex with her, you'd be out of luck. "He couldn't even pay my damn phone bill for me."

"Girl, you got money."

One thing about Lea, she had her own money, but she just preferred to spend a guy's money. She felt as if a man wanted to fuck, he was going to have to spend some money.

"So?" she said with an attitude. "I wanna spend their money, not mine." She was serious. "I got to teach you some of my tricks."

There I was, 22 years old and had never had sex a day in my life. I had sex toys out of this world, though. I just hadn't found *the one* yet. "You need sex in your life," Lea said fixing her make-up.

"It'll happen one day."

"Bitch, you gon' be a 40-year-old virgin," she said as we both laughed. We both finished getting dressed and headed to the concert.

The crowd was full, you could barely see the stage. Good thing we had floor seats. Gucci Mane brought the city together that night and I was ready to enjoy every moment of it. Once inside, we ran into King. He was drinking shots with his friends. Lea pulled me towards them. "Hey, King."

"What's up?" He looked at me. "Hey Laylani," he said. I just smiled and waved.

Lea's hip bumped me causing me to lose my balance. King grabbed my arm and pulled me close to him. His cologne had me in a daze. "You good, ma?"

I cleared my throat, "I'm ok."

I looked over at Lea and she was engaged in a conversation with one of the guys that was with King. She was pressing her breast up against him while smiling into his eyes. He started whispering something in her ear and she bit her bottom lip. I shook my head because Lea was so wild. The concert was about to start, so King guided me to our seats that were closed to the stage. Once Gucci Mane got on the stage, the crowd got loud. The screams, applauses, and head bobbing let me know that it was a good vibe in the atmosphere. King's friends were behind us bobbing their heads to the music and dancing. I looked around, and there was no sign of Lea.

"Where's Lea?" I yelled over the music at King. He bent down to bring his ear closer to my mouth. He came a little too close because my lips hit his ear. "Where's Lea?" I asked again.

"I don't know," he yelled back. He focused back on the concert while I stood there looking around for her. I wondered where she could be. She knew not to leave me with a stranger. I just shrugged my shoulders and focused on the concert. I wasn't about to let my money go to waste by not enjoying myself due to worrying prematurely.

CHAPTER TWO

Lea

Once we bumped into King and his friends, his home boy instantly eyed me. He walked up to me and asked my name. I told him, and he introduced himself as Kane. He was fine as hell. He looked like 'Money' was his middle name.

My eyes wandered down to his manhood; I could see it through his pants. His smile had me in a daze. He had perfect white teeth and the body of a damn god. My juices were flowing for all of him. He asked if I smoked, and I said yes.

We walked to the car, sat inside, and rolled two blunts. My mouth watered for just a small taste of him. I licked my lips at the sight of him sitting in the driver side of his Cadillac Escalade while I was on the passenger side.

"So, Lea, where you from?" He asked.

"Here, in Atlanta."

"Oh, for real?"

The way he worked his tongue while licking the blunt was making my pussy moist. I couldn't fight the temptation anymore. I reached over, grabbed his hands, and placed them on my lap. I unzipped his pants and exposed his manhood. My eyes widened at the sight of his big, juicy penis. My mouth was more than ready to find out what it tasted like. Eager, I placed my mouth over his dick and didn't stop lowering my head until I could feel its tip tap the back of my throat.

"Shit!" he moaned. His hand was on the back of my head, pushing it up and down. I didn't give a damn that I had just met the guy.

"You only live once," I thought.

Growing up, my mom, Cynthia, taught me how to hustle men. She taught me that pussy was power and that it ruled the world. She always reminded me that with a blessing like pussy in between my legs, I should never go broke. We never called her mama or mom like other kids called their mother. We called her "CJ", short for Cynthia Johnson, which she preferred us to do. She said that it made her feel young. I never mind calling her CJ, she was not a mother figure to me to be called Mom anyway.

When I was younger, she would have me sleep with her men for money. By the time I was 15, I was fucking and sucking, and knew everything there was to know about sex. It wasn't my fault. I didn't want to grow up fast, but CJ was selfish, only caring about herself. All she did was get high on drugs, get drunk, and made me and my sister, Ciara, sleep with men for money for her sake. Lani was so much different than I. She was a virgin at 22 and I was most definitely not one. In fact, I never understood how she hung out with me. Everybody knew I was a hoe because of the stories that were told around town; but I got my respect though. Both men and women knew to respect me when they saw me in the street. I was not scared of no one and they knew that I was not scared to fight or have your ass beat.

"Damn, girl," he groaned as I forced his dick to the back of my throat, moving my head from side to side letting him feel my throat. "You sucking this dick so good!"

I pulled off of it and wrapped my lips around the tip of his head and played with it with my tongue. I went down and licked his balls and spit on his head and licked it up again. I looked up at him and his head was laid back on the headrest. I could feel the vein in his dick and knew he was about to bust. My moans mixed in with his, and my pussy was getting wetter by the minute.

"Ahhhh!" I could feel him shaking and I knew he was about to nut. "I'm about to cum all in your mouth, girl."

He still had his hand on the back of my head, fucking my mouth. Then he bust in my mouth, and I swallowed his cum like it was water. I then spit some out onto his dick and licked it back up. I could feel him getting weak in the seat. His body slid down as he breathed heavily. I sat up and smiled as I licked my lips. "Damn, girl."

"I had to taste you."

"Let's get out of here," he suggested. "Fuck that concert."

"Let me shoot my girl a text, and we can go to my crib."

"Cool." He started the truck up and we headed to my place. I felt bad leaving Lani alone with King, but she was a grown woman. Plus, I knew she'd forgive me.

As we walked into the apartment, I slipped my shoes off and jumped into Kane's arm. He lifted me up and I wrapped my legs around him while he carried me into the bedroom. Our kisses felt passionate, which was weird being that we had just met. His strong muscular arms felt good to my body. As we bust into my room, Kane threw me onto the bed. I ripped my clothes off, and he did the same. Kane pulled me to the end of the bed, and I unzipped his pants to release the beast he had between his legs. I worked my magic once again until he came in my mouth.

Once I was done, Kane grabbed a condom and placed it on his dick, which I was fiending for at this point. He lifted my legs over his shoulders and smiled at my vagina as it shined at him. He dove his face into my pussy, and my moans were loud and sexy. My voice filled the room as Kane ate me out like I was his last meal. His tongue felt so good to me. Out of all the guys I had been with, Kane was by far the best. I was feeling so amazing as he licked my pussy like his life depended on it. I grabbed his head because I couldn't take the pleasure anymore. He pushed my hands away and pinned them down. Kane was pleasing the hell out of me. I thought he was going to slurp *all* of my juices up. Finally, after my third time climaxing, Kane wiped my juices from his chin and rammed his beast inside of me.

My body shook as he stroked in and out of me. Kane had my body doing things that I never thought it could do. I had never felt like this before. "Kane," I moaned.

"You like that shit?" By that time, he had flipped me over on all fours, slapping my ass.

"Yes! Oh, Kane, I'm about to cum!"

I lost count of my bodily explosions. Kane had me climaxing excessively. I creamed and squirted all over him. He pounded in and out of my pussy, in deep, long strokes. "I can't take it no more!" I screamed in the middle of Kane's strokes. For the first time in my life, I tapped out. Kane didn't listen, though. He flipped over on his back and I rode him until he filled his condom with cum.

"Shit, girl," he grunted once he came.

I laid my head on his chest, breathing hard and heavy. We both fell asleep, and before we realized it, it was 4 o'clock in the morning.

CHAPTER THREE

Laylani

Even though I was mad that Lea had just left me, I still enjoyed my night. King was being nice and all, but I played hard to get, pretending that I was somewhat disinterested.

After the concert, I headed home to shower and go to bed. It was a little after midnight. I figured Lea had company because her shoes were at the front door. Shaking my head at my friend's behavior, I went straight to my room. Once I was tucked in my bed, King sent me a message.

It read, "Good night, beautiful."

I smiled, rolled over and went to sleep without responding.

When I woke the next morning, I smelled breakfast in the air. Lea always cooked breakfast, and I always cooked dinner. I got up to freshen up, and then I headed into the kitchen. Lea was standing at the stove wearing nothing but a black bra and boy shorts. Her ass cheeks poked out from the bottom of the boy shorts.

"Good morning," I greeted her. "You must've had a long night."

"I did!" she offered instantly. "Girl, he didn't leave until 4 this morning."

"Damn," I laughed. "Bitch y'all must was getting it in."

"That's right! And he got money!" She sat my plate of French toast, bacon and eggs in front of me while I poured our glasses of orange juice. "He and his brother both."

"Who? The guy that gave me his number?"

"Yes, girl. Their dad owns a construction company. He's gonna pass it down to them once he retires."

"Damn, he told you all this in one night?"

She nodded.

"Well, you know I don't care about all that. I get my own money."

"But, girl, they're both fine," she said as she sipped her juice.

I just shook my head and ate my breakfast. I had a class at noon, so once I finished eating, I headed to school.

I was in school to obtain a bachelor's degree in business management. I was almost done; I just had to take one more final exam. My mom stayed on my ass about my grades, so my grade point average was a 4.0. Once I had passed my exam, my plan was to open a clothing boutique.

When I arrived at class, I sat in a seat two rows from the front. As soon as I sat down, my phone vibrated; it was King. He told me that he enjoyed my company and wanted to take me out later. I wasn't sure about all of that since I had just met him. Plus, I was convinced that all men only wanted one thing. I was just trying to focus on my schoolwork so that I could get my business degree and then be my own boss.

Once I left school, I headed to the corner store to fill up my gas tank. I had gone into the store to pay for the gas when I bumped into King; my head bumped right into the middle of his chest. He smelled so good. I had to catch myself. Before I knew it, my hands were on his chest trying to push him back a little. His muscles poked out of his shirt.

"Oh, I'm sorry," I snatched my hands back.

He laughed, "Don't apologize." I blushed and walked away.

"Wait!" he called from behind me. "You never texted me back."

"I was busy."

"Well, you're not busy now."

"Look, I don't mean to be rude, but I'm not interested."

I lied.

"Damn, just like that?" He smiled showing off his beautiful white teeth. "We'll meet again, baby girl."

He walked off and got into his truck. Once he was out of my sight, I took a couple of deep breaths. No one had ever made me lose my breath. I was really nervous over a simple conversation.

I paid for my gas, pumped, and headed home.

CHAPTER FOUR

King

Two months ago, I thought I had met the girl of my dreams. I was 28 years old with no kids and ready to settle down. I have had my share of women, and I was looking for somebody to call my own. Laylani had me wanting her bad. She wasn't like any ordinary female; she was bad and beautiful.

My heart skipped a beat when I first approached her. She was looking good standing in that ticket line. I had to say something. I could tell she never had a real man in her life. Her friend, however, looked thirsty as hell as she undressed me with her eyes. My eyes were focused on Laylani, though. Once I introduced myself, she gave in and we exchanged numbers.

Ever since our exchange at the concert, I have been trying to take things to the next level with her. She didn't want to give me the time of day, though.

Once I ran into her at the gas station, her eyes lit up like they did when she saw me for the very first time at the concert. I knew she was feeling me and that she was just playing hard to get.

I was headed to my office to handle some things, but I couldn't really concentrate. My dad, John Wallace, was retiring, and Kane and I were planning a retirement party for him. Kane had our office manager, Sasha, make the calls that would handle all the decor and catering. We had everything under control. My dad was at the age, 60, in which he was tired and was ready to pass the business, K & K Construction, down to Kane and me. Me being the oldest, I would be Kane's boss.

Growing up, it was only my dad, Kane and me in the house. My mom had breast cancer and passed away when we were younger. I hate that I never got a chance to get to know her. I think about it all the time. I miss her so much. I don't have many memories of her either; all I remember is that she used to lay in bed all day, ringing her bell for my dad to come to her side. My dad didn't want us seeing her like that, so he kept us away from her most of the time. We have a few old photos around the house of her when she was younger. Other than the photos, I have no memories of my mom.

I would hear her crying every night. I'm still haunted by the fact that I couldn't do anything to help her because I was so young. Once she died, my dad packed us up and moved us to Atlanta. We were living in Savannah, Ga at the time, where Kane and I were born. He never spoke much about her. He said that he always wanted to just live in the moment.

I finished up at the office and headed home. Once I got there, Kane and Lea were in the living room laying across the sofa, asleep. I shook my head because my brother was wild. Growing up, my pops taught us how to treat a lady right, but not like princesses because he said we'd get hurt in the end. Kane was a sex addict, and he had no respect for women ever since his previous break-up. His ex-girlfriend left him for another woman. He catered to her and did everything he could to demonstrate his love for her. He paid all the bills, made sure that she that she was up to date with all the new fashions, bought her cars, and made sure that her pockets stayed full – everything that a woman could ask for in a relationship. Kane wanted to marry her, but she had other plans. Disappointed at the memory of the situation, I jumped in the shower and headed to bed.

The next day, I headed over to the venue where we were having my dad's party. That night was *the* night, and I was ready to become the boss. After checking on things, I headed to the mall to pick out an outfit for the party. I had never been the last minute type, but I was so focused on making sure the party was perfect that an outfit slipped my mind. Once I found the perfect outfit, I headed home to change. It was already 6:15 p.m., and the party was going to start at 8. I walked in the house and Kane was in the living room smoking a blunt.

"What's up, bro?" he said.

"What's good? Why you not dressed?"

"After I'm done with this, I'm getting dressed."

"Save me a hit."

If you didn't know us, you would have probably thought we were twins. According to our dad and just about everyone else we knew, we looked just alike. Kane was just a little lighter and shorter than me. We were close too. In fact, you would have thought that he didn't have his own place the way he stayed at mine. Both of our homes were custom-built from the ground up, but I wasn't sure what made him enjoy mine more than his own.

After I had gotten dressed, I smoked a few blunts and we headed to the venue at about 7 p.m. The party's theme colors were red and black, so Kane and I dressed accordingly. We both wore black dress pants, red button-down shirts with black bow ties and black dress shoes. I had on my black classic Kangal cap, and Kane just sported a low temp fade.

"I hope you don't mind, but I invited Lea," Kane said.

"Naw, you good. Her friend coming?"

"I don't know."

I nodded my head to the music. A few drinks and songs later, in walked Lea with Laylani. Laylani looked beautiful. The dark purple dress that she wore hugged her hips like a glove. Her hair hung down her back, black and silky looking; it swayed and blew in the wind as she walked. Even with a bare face, she was still the most beautiful woman I have ever laid eyes on. She and Lea walked in our direction near the bar and stopped right in front of us.

"What's up, y'all?" Lea greeted us.

"What's good?" I replied.

"You remember my girl, Laylani?" She looked at me.

"And we meet again," I kissed the back of her hand. "Didn't I tell you?"

She yanked her hand away, "Boy, please."

I laughed, "Would you like something to drink?"

"I'll buy my own," she snapped. Her attitude only

made me want her even more.

"Well, can I lead you to the bar?"

She rolled her eyes, "Fine."

Laylani and I walked towards the bar with Kane and Lea on our heels. I ordered a Corona and she ordered a margarita. As soon as we ordered, my dad started speaking over the mic.

"I would like to thank everyone who came out to help me celebrate my retirement. I would like to give a special thanks to my boys, Kingston and Kannon. They played a big part in all of this. Without them, I don't know where I'd be. And my best friend, Elroy Matthews, who has been my one true friend since I moved here from Savannah. He's been like a brother that I have never had. "Thanks, Bro," he tilted his glass towards Elroy. "Let's turn the music back up and continue this party. Thanks, again. I love y'all," he lifted his glass up aiming towards Kane and me. The DJ turned the music back up and everyone started dancing to the music. Since my dad was older, the DJ made sure to play old school music, but he mixed tunes from back in the day with a little mixture of today's music.

The party was held at a local hotel ballroom, so if guests got too drunk or horny, they could get a room.

The company office manager, who arranged everything, tried to make it convenient.

Inside the ballroom was like walking into a garden of black balloons and red roses, which were my mother's favorite flowers. The dry-ice smoke swirled over the dance floor as two or three of my dad's workers and their wives were dancing to a string of Maze featuring Frankie Beverly tunes. The old school music played softly in the background while everyone enjoyed the food and mingled. After about an hour, I signaled for the DJ to turn up the music to encourage everyone to dance.

We were sitting at the head table with my father in the center. I kept eyeing Laylani to see if any men were coming up to the table where she and Lea where sitting with a few other people.

"Wanna dance?" I asked Laylani over the music.

"I'm good," she fanned me off. "I'm just gonna sit here and sip on my Moscato." She was on her third drink.

"Don't you think you should slow down?"

"I'm a big girl."

She was so beautiful, sitting across from me looking like the late singer Aaliyah. Her long, beautiful hair was looking silky and soft. I couldn't help but to want her more. Her resistant attitude was turning me on too. I mean, I'm a man before anything, and Laylani had me harder than a rock.

"When are you going to give me a chance to take you out?"

She sipped her wine, "I barely know you."

"That's part of getting to know somebody."

"I'll think about it."

"Just let me have this dance, please."

I could tell that the alcohol was kicking in. "Just one dance."

She placed her hand into mine while I led her to the dance floor. The dress that she had on hugged her slim-thick physique so well. Her heels didn't make her seem much taller, but they looked so good on her freshly pedicured feet.

As we danced to the music, R. Kelly's *Slow Dance* played through the speakers, I noticed that she had the moves. She grinded her hips on me while I held onto her waist. I had to keep my composure, though. I had to get to know this girl more. She would give in sooner or later; I just knew it.

CHAPTER FIVE

Kane

Since I had met Lea, we had been fucking like hell. My manhood was sore from all the sex we had had, but I enjoyed every moment of it. I hadn't been this involved with anybody since Tara walked out on me. She left me for a woman, which had me feeling low. I thought that I, or maybe my sex, wasn't good enough. I brought home the money, I paid the bills, and I even cooked. I couldn't figure out what more she could have wanted. We had broken up two years prior to me meeting Lea, and I had been sleeping with a different girl every chance I got. I promised myself that there would be no feelings involved- only sex. The way Lea had me feeling, made me want to change my mind. She had me in love- at least with her pussy. She was bad, and regardless of her history, I still wanted to be with her.

King and I had been running shit since our dad's retirement. His retirement party went just as planned. Everybody enjoyed themselves, including my dad. He had finally been freed from working. He could sit around on his ass all day while still collecting money.

Lea and I were chilling at my place. We were just laying around, chilling, watching Netflix when a bang on the door caused me to jump. It was 10 p.m. I wondered who in the hell could have been knocking like the police at this time of night. As I got closer to the door, I eased my gun out of its holster. As I turned the knob, I swung the door open with my gun pointed to the person's head.

"What the fuck you doing here?" I asked angrily.

It was my ex, Tara. She stood there looking a beautiful, hot mess. Her makeup was smeared like she had been crying. "I need you," she cried out.

She had some nerve. I hadn't heard from or seen this woman in two years, and out of nowhere, she decided to show up at my doorstep. I was so caught off guard by her being there that I initially didn't even notice the kid standing next to her.

"What do you want and why are you here?" I placed the gun back in the holster and stepped onto the porch.

"This is your daughter, Madison," she said as if that news hadn't been totally unexpected. "My girl is tired of taking care of your daughter. You need to be a man. She needs her father in her life."

Those words had me stuck. "Get the fuck out of here," I said with a look of disgust. "I haven't seen you in two years and suddenly I have a daughter? Bitch, get off my doorstep and go find your child's father."

I stepped back into the house and slammed the door in her face. I felt bad because at one point in time, Tara was my everything. Seeing her at my doorstep brought back so many old memories. She was still a beautiful woman with a dark brown, smooth, silky skin. She always made me melt whenever I penetrated her. She never wore her real hair, though. She always kept that Brazilian weave shit in it.

I walked back into the house, and it was hard for me to look at Lea because I was having mixed emotions about my ex.

"Who was that?" she asked me.

"Nobody," I lied.

"Nobody had you at the door for a while."

"Let's just drop it, Lea. We'll talk about it later."

I headed upstairs for bed. I had some thinking to do. How the fuck did Tara expect me to think that that kid was mine? I mean, the little girl *did* look like she might have been around the age of 2, though. I shook the thoughts from my mind and took a shower. Once I was out, Lea was sitting at the foot of the bed with her arms folded.

"Who was she?" she asked me in a way that let me know she wanted answers immediately.

I stood at the doorway with my head hanging low, "My ex, Tara."

"Why was she here?"

"She said that I have a daughter."

"How? You said you haven't seen her in two years."

"I know. The little girl looks around that age."

I could tell she was hurt.

"It's only one way to find out."

"I'll handle it," I said as I walked towards the bed.

I lifted Lea's head up and kissed her passionately. She pulled the towel down from my waist, exposing my manhood. My inches stood straight up between her eyes. I loved the way her eyes glossed whenever she laid them on my dick. Lea was a pro at what she did, and I loved it. She placed her mouth over my dick, covering the whole thing. I could feel her throat while I fucked her mouth. Lea had no gag reflexes, so it felt like I was actually fucking her. The shit felt so good that I busted in just a few minutes.

Lea then turned over on all fours, exposing that pretty, pink pearl. She told me about her past, but it made no difference because her wet hole fit my dick like a glove. I slid right on in it, slow stroked it, sped up, then started slowly again. Lea's moans made me even harder. I couldn't help myself; I was about to bust.

"Don't cum yet, baby," she moaned. "I wanna taste it again."

That shit had me weak in the knees. Lea knew just what to do to ease my mind. After she swallowed, I lit a blunt and we smoked until we both were high and fell asleep.

CHAPTER SIX

Lea

Me and Kane had been messing around for a little over two months now. Everything had been going good until his ex, Tara, showed up again. I could tell that Kane was hurt by her leaving because I could see it in his eyes. I couldn't get mad, though, because she was his girl before I was. I just hated the thought of having to step up to be some child's stepmother. I knew nothing about kids. I had to call my girl to let her in on what was going on. We decided to head to the mall to talk.

"Are you serious?" Laylani asked. "So, what he gon' do?"

"He said he'll handle it."

"I sure hope so. This is too much. Y'all just started talking a few months ago."

"Speaking of a few months ago, why haven't you given King a chance yet?"

"You know I'm trying to focus on my schoolwork."

"Bitch, you got a 4.0 grade point average. A little fun won't hurt."

"You're right, but I get butterflies when I'm around him. I be nervous."

"I'm gonna set y'all up on a date."

"Don't do that. I got it."

"You better. I'm gon' have to teach you a few things."

"Girl, please," she fanned me off.

"I'm hungry. Let's grab something to eat."

Laylani and I were at the food court getting ready to order food when some chick walked up to us with three girls standing behind her. She was standing with a group of girls with her hand on her hip.

"Uh, I was standing here first," she smacked her lips.

"We didn't see nobody when we walked up," I snapped at her.

"Bitch," she started, before I cut her off.

"You don't know me, so I suggest you get up out my face."

"You better let her know, Lea," Laylani said standing next to me.

"Look, I don't know what kind of games y'all playing or the lies Kane is telling you, but he's my man and I'm coming back home."

Once she said that, I figured it was the chick from the

other day that was at his doorstep. I laughed so hard you would have thought that I was at a comedy show.

"Girl, get out my face with that drama," I shrugged. "Don't try and think you can just pop up and come back into his life. That's my man, baby, and he's not going anywhere."

She rolled her eyes and stepped up in my face. "Oh I'm coming home," she said, "and you better be gone."

Once she said the word "gone," I blacked out, dropped my bags on the floor and punched the bitch in her face. The girls who were with Tara all jumped in to attack me. Laylani was right by my side, though. I could hear her telling them to let us fight one on one, but they weren't trying to hear that.

Once I had the bitch pinned on the floor, I looked up and saw Laylani going at it with two of the girls who were with Tara. She was handling herself though.

Tara pulled my hair, which caught me off guard. She snatched me up after rolling over on top of me. There was a crowd gathering around recording all the action instead of trying to break the fight up. Although Tara had me on the ground, I was still throwing blows to her face. Meanwhile, one of the girls with her was kicking me in my side.

Finally, security came running up to stop the fight.

"Don't think this is over!" Tara yelled as we were being

escorted out the building at separate exits.

Security warned us, "If y'all don't get away from here, I'm calling the police."

They threw our bags at us and walked back into the mall. Laylani and I walked towards the car. Tara and her crew hopped in their rides and sped off.

Once in the car, Laylani spoke first. "Bitch, what the fuck?" She was looking in the mirror at her busted lip.

"Girl, I have no idea. I don't know where they came from. How do she know what I look like? I can't wait to tell Kane about this shit."

I drove 100 mph all the way to Kane's house. He was going to have to explain to me what the hell was going on. Once we got to his place, Laylani sat in the living room while I headed upstairs. Kane was laying on the bed watching TV.

"What the fuck happened to your face?" He sat up on the bed.

"That bitch Tara!" I stood at the door with my hands on my hips. My nose was bleeding, and my lip was busted. "How does she know me?" I asked him. "Lani and I were at the mall, and she and a group of girls walked up out of nowhere and jumped us. She said that she was coming home to you, and I better not be here. And she said that you're lying to me about something." Before I knew it, an actual tear was running down my face. I couldn't believe it.

"Lea, baby, don't cry," he said.

"Get your hands off me!" I pushed him away. "Handle that bitch!"

I stormed into the bathroom to wash my face. "This bitch has some nerve," I thought.

CHAPTER SEVEN

Laylani

Lea and her drama had me so thrown off. I had never expected to be in a fight with anybody over a man, especially about one that wasn't mine. The only man I could seem to think about was King. I had gone out with a few other guys, but those situations never got too serious. Either they were broke men claiming to have big dicks or well off men claiming to have "big plans" for us, but they were all dogs. I am glad that I never went there with them and still have my virginity. Frustrated and curious, I decided to give King a chance since I was sort of digging him.

I had my plan all figured out. I was going to accidentally bump into him on purpose and let him offer to take me out. Since it seemed like we were always running into each other every Monday evening after my class at the gas station, I planned to wait there in my car until his truck pulled up.

Once I saw his truck, I fixed myself up and stepped out

of the car. I made sure to wear something nice so I could get his attention. I had on some high waisted jean shorts with a nude halter top and nude heels. My hair hung down my back and my nude lipstick was popping.

As I walked into the store, I acted like I didn't see him. I walked down the aisle to grab something. He was on the phone with somebody, so I kept acting like I was looking for something. I sensed him walking toward my direction. I felt my clitoris jump in his presence. I couldn't help myself.

"Hey, beautiful," he said making me with a smirk. He always smelled so good. I could bite him right now. "Why is it that we always meet up here at the same time every Monday? You stalking me?"

I laughed, "Boy, please." I continued acting like I was looking for something.

He laughed. "Let's go out for dinner; it's on me."

"Dinner?" I smacked my lips.

"Yes, you don't like to eat?" He asked while smiling.

I laughed, "Of course I do."

"Well, let me take you out. You think that this is a coincidence that we keep bumping into each other every Monday around the same time?"

I rolled my eyes, playing hard, "That is all that it is, a coincidence."

He laughed, showing off his gorgeous smile, "Baby girl,

this is fate. You are going to be my wife one day."

"Oh, yeah?" I blushed.

"Hell yeah. You'll see," he said. "So, can I take you out or not?"

"Dressed the way I am?"

"You're beautiful. You look good in anything."

"Okay," I whined. "How about Saturday?"

"How about Friday?"

I thought about it for a minute because I didn't want to seem so desperate. "Friday it is."

"See you Friday at 7."

He turned to walk off. I waited for him to pump his gas before I walked out to my car, got in, and headed over to my mom's. I was kind of excited about going on a date. I hadn't been out in a while. I had been so focused on school that I just stopped dating. I figured going to dinner wouldn't hurt anything, though; it was just a date. Besides, I had needed to loosen up anyway. I wasn't getting any younger.

I pulled up to my mom's house and parked my car next to hers. She and my dad were hardworking like me. My mom was a registered nurse at the office where my dad had his family medical practice. They had been married since before I was born, for nearly 30 years. I was spoiled growing up because I was an only child, I never went without anything; they always hustled for the life that they lived. Whatever they wanted, they got.

I slid my key into the knob, turned it, and pushed the door open. Once I closed the door, I could hear my dad snoring from upstairs. I smiled and walked into the kitchen, where my mom was.

"Hey, mom!" I hugged her and kissed her on the jaw. Her Asian skin was soft and smooth.

"Hey, baby," she kissed my jaw back. She was cooking lasagna, which was my dad's favorite. "How's school?"

"Everything's good. I took my last final exam and passed it. Just waiting on graduation now."

"Why haven't you said anything about passing the exam? That's something to celebrate."

"To be honest, mom, I'm used to passing tests. It didn't faze me."

"Girl, you're crazy."

"How's work?"

"As you can see, it's wearing your dad out," she laughed. "He can't get a break even if he asked for it. Today is our first *real* day off in three months."

"Wow, I don't wanna be that busy."

"That comes with being your own boss. You think you can just call out when you want to but you gotta keep the place running."

"You're right," I grabbed a bottled water from the refrigerator.

"Are you dating yet?"

"There's this guy I'm interested in, but nothing serious right now. I met him a few months ago, and we're going on a date, Friday."

"Good, you need to get out more. School keeps you so drained and pre-occupied. You need some fun." She started dancing as if there was music playing.

"Mom! Stop," I laughed.

After eating and chatting with my mom, I kissed her and my dad good-bye, and I headed home. Once I was there, I showered and then climbed into bed to watch TV. I was excited for Friday; I was ready to see what this date was going to be like.

Before I knew it, the day had arrived. I let Lea know so she could stop jumping down my damn throat about dating. She always told me that I needed to stop being stuck up, because I could be running my potential husband away. After scanning through the closet, I finally picked out what I wanted to wear. I decided on my blue jean romper that stopped right above my knees. My hair was up in a bun and on my feet were my nude flats that tied up my legs. My ass was sitting just right in my romper. I made sure that my makeup was perfect. I even wore a nude lipstick shade to match my shoes.

King arrived at 6:45; I had been ready since 6:30. He stepped out of his black Range Rover and walked to my door. He looked damn good. Once I opened the door, he handed me a dozen red roses. "Hey beautiful," he said with that sweet grin he always had on his face whenever he would greet me. I smelled the roses and smiled. He grabbed my hand and led me to the car. He opened the door for me and I got in. We headed to downtown Atlanta. King was wearing a fitted black t-shirt that showed off his muscles, black jeans and black Jordan sneakers. The fragrance of his cologne had me mesmerized. His *car* even smelled good; this man was like a god—he could do no wrong.

Once we arrived at Phipps Plaza, King got out and opened my door. The valet guy parked the car while we he guided me to a restaurant inside, Grand Lux Café, where he had made reservations. King pulled my chair out for me; he was being such a gentleman.

"How was your day?" he asked after the waitress brought our drinks out. I ordered sweet tea and he ordered a coke. After she placed our drinks on the table, I ordered a grilled house salad while King ordered Ribeye steak and baked potato.

"Well, I didn't have class, so it was okay."

"How long do you have left in school?"

I sipped my drink. "I graduate in a few weeks."

"Well, congratulations," he said sounding genuinely happy. "What's your major?"

"Business management."

"Oh, okay. That's what's up."

"How's the business going? You know… since your dad's retirement."

"Everything's good. Money coming, so I can't complain."

I nodded my head and looked away. The waitress brought our food to our table and we ate and chatted more. "So, do you want to get married and have kids one day?"

"One day," I said, somewhat shocked by the question. "Once I find my prince charming."

He laughed, "I'm right here, baby."

That made me laugh as well. "How old are you?"

"Twenty-eight, baby girl."

"Okay, I'm 22. I've never dated a guy older than me. We've always been the same age."

"Well, there's a first time for everything."

"It'll most definitely be my first time," I thought to myself.

We chatted more and ended our evening by giving each other a kiss on the cheek. King was everything I had been looking for. Other guys were rude and just straight up nasty, but King was different. I enjoyed my date, and I was ready for another one.

CHAPTER EIGHT

King

After my date with Laylani, I was ready to make her my lady. She was such a lady, and she didn't take mess from nobody. She looked so good, and she had some business about herself. My dad taught me how to treat a lady. I had been taught all about opening doors and pulling out seats and holding hands. I just hoped she would let me take her out again.

Kane and I were at his place chilling with the guys. We were all smoking blunts and drinking Remy and Hennessey. I could tell that my brother was stressed. He didn't show his emotions, but I knew my brother.

Kane and I were sitting at the bar talking while the other guys were playing pool. He was bobbing his head to Gucci's new mixtape, *The State vs Radric Davis,* as he pulled on the blunt. "Man, Tara is bugging."

I *knew* something was wrong! "What's going on now?" I asked him.

"We did the DNA test. Madison is mine. I'm happy but mad at the same time. Like how can you get pregnant and leave, then pop up two years later? And not tell me shit?"

"How does Lea feel about all of this?"

"Bruh, she don't even know yet. I hate to bring drama in. Our relationship just got serious."

"I hear you baby boy, but you can't keep this a secret. She's your girl, and Madison is your daughter. Now you gotta step up and do what you got to do," I told him. "You know Pops been waiting for a grand baby. You gotta take her to see him."

"You're right, bruh."

We continued to smoke and drink. I was still in shock my damn self. I couldn't believe Tara would do some shit like that. That girl was everything to my brother at one point in time.

I left there and headed home. On the way there, my phone kept vibrating in my pocket. To my surprise, I saw multiple texts and calls from my ex. I couldn't understand what the fuck was so important to make her text and call me over and over again.

I opened the texts and saw pictures of ultrasounds, which read: "Congratulations on your baby boy." I kept scrolling and the bitch said she was excited to have my baby. She was out her rabbit ass mind thinking that she was pregnant by me. I hadn't touched that girl in months, and when we were having sex, we always used condoms. Still, I decided to call her.

"Hey, baby," she sang into the phone.

"Ciara, what the fuck, man?"

"What? Aren't you excited?" she asked. "I was gonna have a gender reveal party, but I couldn't wait to tell you."

"Ciara, are you serious right now? I haven't touched you in months. What makes you think that's my baby?"

"Kingston, baby, it only takes one time to make a baby. I love you. What's wrong?"

"What's wrong? What's wrong is you calling me with this bullshit knowing that's not my baby. I even wore a rubber when I fucked you. Don't bring this shit to me like we all in love. Miss me with that shit, man."

I could tell she was smiling from the other end of the phone. "But, Kingston, he's your son. We've always talked about having your son."

"I'm gonna need a DNA test, Cee."

"How dare you act like this isn't your baby?" She was yelling into the phone. "Nigga, you know this is your son; it was planned. You knew I was out of town taking care of things for my mom all these months. Don't act like you didn't know."

"I don't wanna have anything to do with yo' ass, you trifling bitch."

She was quiet, but finally broke the silence.

"Ok, you wanna play?" That was the last thing she said before she hung up.

Ciara was my girl before I met Laylani. She was everything a nigga could have asked for until I caught her in bed with another man. She had some nerve saying that baby was mine when we hadn't been together since before she cheated. I kicked her ass out of my house, and she went to stay with her mom down in Savannah, Ga. She thought that I was going to fall for her trick, but I wasn't a damn fool.

I pulled into my driveway, got out, and headed inside. I was so pissed at how Ciara was coming at me. I decided to call Laylani and talk to her.

"Hello?" she said sexily.

"I missed you."

I could hear her smiling. "That's sweet King."

"Damn, you don't miss me?" I laughed.

She was still smiling. "I do want to see you again."

"Let's make this happen, baby girl."

"You want to come over? Watch a few movies? Popcorn?"

"I'll be there soon."

We hung up. I hopped in the shower and threw on some jogging pants and a tank top. I grabbed my Nike slides on my way out the door. Once I arrived at Laylani's place, I stepped out and headed to the door. Before I could even knock, Laylani swung the door open. She was standing with a big t-shirt on with some tights on underneath. Her hair was in a bun, and she wasn't wearing any makeup. She still looked beautiful, though.

"You look beautiful in anything," I said as I admired her beauty.

"Thanks. You don't look too bad yourself."

I followed her to the living room where we cuddled on the couch. We watched a few movies and ate popcorn until she fell asleep. Her head was on my shoulder and I heard a slight snore coming from her mouth. I smiled at the sight of this gorgeous woman that was lying next to me. I picked her up and put her in bed. She rolled right over and went back to sleep. I tucked her in, kissed her forehead and went back home.

The next morning, I went to Kane's office. When I walked in, he had his feet propped up on his desk. "Yeah, that's what's up. I'll hit you back," he said as he ended his call. He looked over at me. "What's up, bruh?"

"What's up, what's going on?"

"Oh, nothing, that was Sasha letting me know that I have an interview today at 2:00."

"Who you about to hire on?"

"Some guy named Quan Keyes. He's from…" Kane looked through the application, "…Savannah, Ga."

"Why is he looking for a job up here?"

He shrugged his shoulder, "The hell if I know. I'm gon' check this cat out and see what's up."

"Cool, just hit me up so I can know what to do about hiring him."

"Bet."

I left out of Kane's office and headed upstairs to mine. Once I was in my comfortable in my chair, I propped my feet up on my desk. As soon as I had gotten good and relaxed, in walked the lovely miss Lani. She walked over towards my desk and propped her ass up on its corner.

"Thanks for tucking me in last night," she smiled.

"You're welcome, baby girl. You looked like you need the rest."

"School is draining me. I would love for you to come to my graduation ceremony."

"I would love to," I said as I sat back in my chair. "When is it?"

"Two weeks. It's on a Saturday, at 12 noon."

"I'm there!"

"Thanks. See you later."

I bit my bottom lip as Laylani walked out of my office.

"That girl is going to be my wife one day," I thought to myself. *"Watch."*

CHAPTER NINE

Kane

I sat at my desk, waiting for my 2:00 p.m. appointment to show. This man had the nerve to walk in 30 minutes late. I was already mad about the games Tara was playing and now, I had to deal with this shit.

Q sat across the desk with his hands over his face looking embarrassed. He was 45 years old, but hard living had him looking much older. His hands were calloused, lips charred from smoking, the whites of his eyes had a yellow tint, and his short beard was filled with streaks of gray. "Man, I'm so sorry," he began. "My wife had me running around doing things for her. She's on bed rest; she's carrying my son. Please forgive me. I need this job."

I sat up and looked him dead in his eyes. "Why should we hire you?"

"Well, I grew up learning how to build and repair things. My dad was always fixing things around the house. I'm the oldest of my siblings and it was me who stepped up once my dad passed. His death took a toll on my mom. I was the one fixing things around the house and doing the cooking and the cleaning."

I nodded while rubbing my chin, "Ok, I see. I have to talk to boss man and see what he says. With you being late, that looks bad on you."

"I know, and I apologize, seriously. It'll never happen again," he promised.

After the interview ended, I went into King's office. Laylani had just walked out, "Hey, Kane."

"What's up?" She closed the door going on about her business.

"Q was late," I told King. I sat across from him at his desk.

"Being late for an interview does not look good," he said as he sat back in his chair. "What was his excuse?"

"Something about his wife being pregnant on bed rest, and he had to do some running around for her."

"That's no excuse, man. If he wanna work, he gotta be on time."

"But his history shows that he knows a lot about construction."

I handed King Q's file. He had plenty of construction experience.

"See if he's willing to travel if we need him. He's not getting another chance. The first time he's late, that's it!"

I nodded my head at my brother's response. He was right.

We ended our discussion, and then I called Tara. We needed to get to the bottom of our situation. Since Madison was my daughter, we needed to come to an agreement about co-parenting. Lea was my girl, and she deserved better than a man who wasn't willing to raise his child. I was going to show her that I was all she'd ever need in a man.

When I arrived at the address Tara gave me, I parked my car and got out. I headed towards the door. Tara opened the door before I had a chance to knock.

I stepped inside, and she closed the door behind us.

"Where's my daughter?" I curiously asked.

"She's upstairs asleep."

"We need to talk." I sat down on the couch across from her.

"What's up?"

"Don't you ever disrespect my girl like that again. What we have or had going on is over. If it's not about Madison, then don't call me."

"The nerve of you to try and come check me about a bitch."

"Watch your mouth." I cut Tara off.

"Fuck you, Kane!"

"Fuck me? No, fuck you! You're the one who walked out on us two years ago then show up with my daughter that I knew nothing about. You could at least have told me that you were pregnant with my child. Now you're sitting here acting like you're the victim when I did everything for you girl!" My emotions took over. I wasn't crying, but I was pissed all over again. She had the nerve to come at me like all the drama and chaos had been my fault. "Now you trying to raise my seed around this gay shit!" I yelled at her. That slipped; I didn't have anything against homosexuals. It just hurt knowing that she left me for another woman.

"Kane, get out my house, right now!" she yelled.

I looked over toward the stairs to see Madison; she was crying. I walked over to her and picked her up. I thought she would resist since she didn't know me, but she came right to me with ease.

"Give me her!" She snatched her from my arms, which made her cry harder.

"Look, let me be a part of my daughter's life. I don't have time for the games you're trying to play."

"I don't want my daughter around that bitch!"

"Stop calling my girl a bitch."

"Whatever, get out!"

"This isn't over!" I said before slamming the door behind

me. I needed to contact my lawyer, because this bitch was going to cause big problems.

CHAPTER TEN

Lea

Ever since Kane had found out that Madison was his daughter, things have been awkward between us. In the end, Tara simply don't want me around her daughter. But it was time to put all the bullshit to the side and confront her to see what the problem was. After all, I did owe her an ass whooping.

As I pulled up to her house, I saw Kane leaving. I ducked down in my seat so he that he would not see me. Once he drove off, I pulled into the driveway. I walked up to the door, and Tara swung it open. Once we stood face to face, I grabbed her face and passionately kissed her. She grabbed the back of my head and guided me into the house, kissing me back.

"Oooh, Lea, baby I've missed you so much," she moaned.

"Where's Madison?" I asked while sucking her neck.

"She's upstairs." I lifted her shirt above her head and unfastened her bra. Her perky nipples stood hard. I grabbed a mouth full of her breast and sucked them nice and slow. Her moans were soft and sexy. “Mmmm, Lea!”

“Lay down,” I commanded her. She walked backwards towards the sofa. “Spread those legs for me and let me see my pussy.”

Yeah, I said it, *my* pussy. I dove in with my tongue and licked her juice box like it was my last meal. Tara always tasted so sweet. I didn’t know if it had something to do with the food she was eating or what. Whatever it was, I hoped that she kept doing it.

Tara grabbed the back of my head and pulled my hair. “I’m about to cum, baby!” She was shaking. I knew she was about to bust, so I slid my fingers into her tight, wet hole. Her moans became a little louder. “Lea!” I looked up and she was biting her bottom lip. “Baby,” she said with pleasure, “Here I come!” She squirted all in my mouth and creamed on my fingers. I licked it off my fingers and kissed her one last time.

“Damn, girl. That pussy always good to me,” I said sitting next to her.

“How long is this going to take? I miss having you around. Now I gotta share you with my baby daddy.”

“Chill out, man. Everything’s gonna be alright. You know

I'm only doing this for the money."

"I know, but it's taking too long."

"Be patient with me, baby. After he gets custody of Madison, I'm leaving him, and we can go on about our lives."

"Ok, I'm sorry about the fight at the mall. I didn't mean to hit you so hard."

"Just don't let it happen again."

"You got my word," she said. "I love you, Lea."

"I love you, too."

We laid there, together, and chatted for the rest of the night. I had the best of both worlds.

CHAPTER ELEVEN

Laylani

Things between King and I had been going great. The time that we had spent with each other was wonderful. King was such a gentleman; his dad raised him right. He opened doors for me, massaged my body after long days, drew my bath water, and he even cooked for me. It's safe to say that I was falling for him. I had never felt this way before. After I graduated, we spent even more time with each other and finally made our relationship official.

After we had spent six months together, I wanted to do something nice for King. He had always been nice to me, smothering me with gifts and catering to me; and he was very patient. I figured that it was about time for me to reciprocate the behavior. When I finally decided what I was going to do for him, I made a run to the mall to grab something sexy. I had decided that I was going to be intimate with King, for the first time, on our six-month anniversary. I was almost 23 years old, and I had never felt the real deal. My body was calling for him. My sex toys were getting old, and my body couldn't take anymore temptation. I wanted King and I needed him.

I prepped the place for his arrival. I had candles all over the place and I had rose petals in a line from the door to the kitchen and up the stairs to the bedroom. I slipped on my Victoria's Secret bra and panty set. King's favorite colors were red and gold, so I made sure I match the colors. My bra and panties were both trimmed in gold, and I had on my red pumps. I sprayed my body with my *Heat*, by Beyoncé, fragrance. King loved that smell.

I could hear King sticking his key in the door. My heart skipped a beat as the door crept open. When the door swung open, and I greeted King with passionate kisses. He didn't resist. He picked me up and wrapped his strong arms around me. I wrapped my legs around his waist. Our kisses seemed to last forever.

"Happy six-month anniversary, baby," I said.

He was still holding onto me.

"Happy anniversary, baby," he replied. I led King to the kitchen, after he let my feet fall back onto the floor, where I had dinner set up on the table. I had prepared steak, baked potatoes, a side salad for our dinner. I had wine in my glass, and I filled his glass with Remy.

"All this for me?" he asked, shocked.

"Don't talk. Tonight is all about you," I smiled.

I fed my man. I catered to him. After we ate, I led him to the tub, which was filled with bubbles. I undressed him and helped him in. I had a few blunts rolled up for him already, so he was good to go. I laid all the blunts on the tub but kept one to light up. King smoked and drank his Remy. He had his head laid back on the tub while I rinsed his body off.

"I love you, Kingston," I sincerely said.

He looked into my eyes and guided me to join him. I began to take my bra and panties off.

"I've loved you since I first laid eyes on you," he replied.

I couldn't help but to smile. I slid into the jacuzzi tub that he had in his bathroom. I'd been staying over a lot, so I was comfortable there. I sat on top of King, and I could feel his hard dick against my soaking wet opening.

"I've never done this before," I whispered in his ear. We kissed passionately as he held me tight.

"I promise to take it slow," he whispered back to me as the tips of his lips grazed my ear.

King then lifted me out the tub and carried me into the bedroom. He laid me down and dried us both off. The night was supposed to be about *me* catering to *him*, but he took over. He planted kisses on my neck and my ears. I felt myself getting moister. I couldn't wait to feel him inside of me.

He then moved his head down to my hard nipples and sucked on them so good that my toes were curled. Then he went down to my stomach and licked circles around my navel. I grabbed the whipped cream from the nightstand and handed it to him. King sprayed my body down with the cream and then licked every bit up. He licked and kissed my inner thigh so softly and gently. I nearly had an orgasm just from that.

King dove into my wetness with his face causing me to rise off the bed like I was possessed. This man had my body doing things that my toys could have never made it do.

"King," I moaned softly. He pushed my hands from his head because I was trying to stop him. He pinned my arms down. My body was shaking. King was licking and sucking my shit so good that I came multiple times. Even though I had come so many times already, he kept going. He flipped me over and licked me from the back. As soon as his tongue touched my asshole, I tried to run, but he caught me and pulled me back to his mouth.

"I can't! King! I can't take no more." He kept licking and sucking causing me to shake and scream with pleasure.

"Baby," I moaned softly. The faces I was making let him know that I was ready for whatever tricks he had coming up next.

He turned me over and looked me into my eyes as he wiped the whipped cream from his face.

"Are you ready?" he sneakily asked. "I'm not gonna hurt you."

The look in his eyes made me fall even more in love with him. I couldn't help but notice his beast standing at attention. Him telling me that he wouldn't hurt me scared me because the size of his manhood was mind-blowing. I just nodded. King placed the condom on and laid on top of me. He planted slow, deep kisses on me and I wrapped my arms around his neck, kissing him back. He then slid his penis into my wet hole. I gasped. I bit down on my lip and rolled my eyes to the back of my head.

"Sssssss! Ahhhhh!" I moaned. "King, baby."

"Want me to stop?" he asked as he kept stroking.

I didn't answer. I kept moaning. My body had never felt so good in my life.

"What the fuck have I been waiting on?" I thought to myself. If I knew sex was this good, I would have *been* getting it in. "Ahh!" King moaned out loud. "I don't wanna nut yet, Lani! This pussy so damn good."

"It's all yours," I whispered in his ear. He pulled out and snatched the rubber off and dove back in. That felt even better. His dick felt harder than before. King flipped me over and went in from the back. I was faced down, ass up. I knew he was about to bust because of the speed at which he was forcing his dick in and out of me. His breathing and moans were louder than mine.

"Lani, baby, ahhhh!"

"Don't stop, King, please!" I begged. I didn't want it to end.

"I'm cumming, girl!" King busted all inside of me. We made love for the rest of the night, over and over again. I felt like I was in heaven. I was glad to have shared my first time with my "king." But it was not over yet, King made love to me over and over again that night. The feeling of being in love with a good man was amazing. I most definitely fell deeper in love that night.

After graduating a few months ago, I immediately began looking for a place to rent for my store. Almost two months later, I had the grand opening of my boutique. I was so proud because it took a little over three months to get everything together.

King had taken care of most everything for the grand opening; I didn't have to worry about much. He even had my hair and makeup appointments ready, and he made sure my wardrobe was nothing less than perfect. The only problem that I was having was a horrible headache and nausea that wouldn't let up.

Thirty minutes before opening time, I was in the dressing room, getting ready to head out, when I took a hard fall. All I could hear was Lea and King yelling over me asking if I was okay. Everything was pitch black.

I woke up in a hospital bed. King was sitting next to my bed, holding my hand. He had his head hanging low. I could hear him mumbling something, though. I looked over on the sofa to see that Lea was on the phone with somebody. I tried lifting my head, but the pounding made it too difficult. I just squeezed King's hand instead.

He looked up at me. "Baby, are you ok?"

"Why am I here, King?"

Lea rushed over to my side. "Lani!"

The doctor walked in, holding a clipboard. "Well, hello, Laylani. I'm Dr. Smith."

"Why am I here?" I asked him. "I need to get back down to my grand opening." I tried to sit up again.

"Ma'am, you need to rest," the doctor told me. "You were dehydrated and that's not good for the baby."

"Baby?" I asked, holding my head.

"Yes, baby, we're having a baby," King kissed my forehead. I smiled.

"We're gonna have to keep you over night, just to keep an eye on the baby," the doctor said. "Congratulations!"

King and I smiled at each other ass the doctor exited the room. He kissed me softly on my lips. "I love you, Lani. Don't scare me like that ever again."

"I know that's right," Lea said.

"I love you, too. I didn't know. It seems like we *just* had sex," I laughed.

"It only takes one time, baby," he said. "You have to take care of yourself, especially now that you're carrying my seed."

"I will baby."

"We had to push your grand opening back to another date. And now that you're carrying my son, I don't want you working, period."

"What makes you think it's a boy?" I smiled.

"I just know."

I was really about to be a mother. I was so excited.

The next day, I was released to go home. King was downstairs waiting for me and Lea; she was pushing me in my wheelchair. I was excited about leaving. I was ready to sleep in my own bed.

When we got home, King stepped out to open my door.

He was so focused on me that he didn't notice the big ass envelope that was attached to the front door. He was still at the car when I walked up to the door. The envelope had both our names written on it in large print. I grabbed it and opened it. Inside were ultrasound photos, so I was happy until I read the letter that had come with them. It read: *Welcome to motherhood, bitch. We're both about to be mothers.*

My smile turned into a frown as I read more. I could hear King calling my name, but I was heated. There was one photo that stood out to me more than any of the others. It read: *'it's a boy'*. Before I knew it, I had turned around and threw the papers in King's face.

"What's this, Kingston?"

He dropped my bags onto the ground and picked up the ultrasound pictures. "Let me explain," he said in hopes of calming me down.

"Explain what? That you have another baby on the way? When were you gonna tell me?"

"Baby."

"Don't baby me," I snatched away from his grip and ran into the house and up the stairs.

"Please, be careful, baby. Sit down and let me explain, please." King took me by the arm and hugged me. I couldn't help but lay my head on his muscular chest.

"Are you gonna hear me out?" he asked.

I took a step back from him with my hands on my hip.

"Explain," I said, even though I really wasn't interested in hearing his excuse right now.

He led me to the bed and we both sat down.

"It's this chick that I was involved with before I met you," he explained. "Her name is Ciara. The bitch is psycho. I haven't seen or heard from her in months. Then you and I met, Lani. When I ended things with her, she busted my windows, flattened my tires, bleached my clothes… and around the same time, her mom got sick. So, she up and left and went to Savannah. A few months ago, I got messages from her saying I'm about to be a father of a son that I know nothing about. So, I told her I wanted a DNA test done."

I shook my head. "Why would you keep this from me, King?"

"I was trying to make sure things were legit first."

I exhaled. "I don't know about this."

"You gotta believe me, Lani. Please believe me." I could hear the truth in his voice as he pleaded with me. "Baby, until the results come back, I'm not speaking to her regarding anything."

I laid my head on his shoulder. "I really hope this is a game. I can't deal with any drama."

"Let me handle this."

He grabbed my chin and kissed me softly. I gave in quickly because his kisses made me weak. King lifted me in his strong arms, laid me on the bed and made love to me. Our night didn't end until the next morning. King put it on me-- made me forget all about that bitch.

CHAPTER TWELVE

King

Ciara had taken taking things too far sending those pictures to my house, knowing that I didn't fuck with her ass like that. I was sitting at my desk when I heard a knock was at my door. Before I even had a chance to welcome her, Ciara walked in and sat across from me. She was indeed pregnant, but that didn't mean the baby was mine. I wasn't claiming any child until I had a DNA test, and she knew that.

"Hey, baby," she said as she sat down. "I've missed you."

"Don't 'hey baby' me. What's your problem? Sending those ultrasounds to my house and then you had the nerve to put my girl's name on it. How the hell do you know her anyway?"

"I have my ways of knowing things," she said with an evil grin on her face.

"I'm not with the games, Cee."

"Look, this is your baby whether you want it to be or not, and you're gonna step up and take care of it."

"DNA, bitch!" I banged my fist onto my desk. "I haven't seen you in months, let alone *touch* yo' ass! Miss me with that shit…"

A knock on the door caused me to pause, mid-sentence.

"Come in," I told the unexpected guest.

In walked Kane and Q. It was Q's first day, and he had come to my office to get his uniform and name tag.

"What's up?" I asked him with an attitude. "This is not a good time."

"Ciara?" Q spoke.

"You know her?" I asked him.

"This is my wife," he said.

I was completely thrown off because this bitch had gotten married and had had the nerve to come to me like her unborn child was mine.

"Wife?" I looked at Ciara sideways, and then she dropped her head.

"Yes, and you're supposed to be on bed rest." Q walked over to her. "Why are you here?"

"To come check on you," she lied. She stood up walking towards him. "I missed you, baby."

I kept my eyes on this bitch the entire time. She rubbed

his face and kissed him. "Now that I know you're okay, I'm gonna leave." She walked out without looking back. Kane looked at me with a look of confusion.

I just shook my head. "Have a seat," I said to Q as I pointed to the chair across from me.

"You know my wife?" Q asked.

"Naw, she was looking for you," I lied. "Kane, give this man his uniform."

I asked Q a few questions and then sent him on his way. Of course, Kane stayed behind to pry.

"What was that about?" he asked me, eager to hear the story behind the awkward moment.

"The bitch swear that the baby is mine. You leave and get married then come back like you never left? I'm not falling for it until I see some test results."

"Boy, the drama we're both carrying around on our shoulders," Kane said.

"What's going on now?"

"I'm fighting for custody of Madison."

"So, you are going through with that?" I asked.

"I don't want to, but it has to be done," Kane said. "I can't have her take her away from me."

"I understand you bro. Do what you got to do man."

"Congratulations, I heard the news."

"Thanks, bro!"

"I'm glad that Lea is here to support a nigga in this mess. She's holding me down."

"That's what's up, I'm happy for you," I told him.

"Just waiting on my lawyer so that we can get started with the case."

"Are you going to give her a chance to explain?" I asked.

"Explain what? How she left me for a woman and was pregnant with my child and did not even bother telling me about it?" Kane fussed.

"Give her a chance to explain what happened and why. You never know what her intentions were."

He exhaled, "I'll think about it. I'm about to head out. You need anything?"

"I'm good. I'm about to head out myself."

"Alright, I'll holla at you!"

Once Kane left, I made a round through the building before I left. Sasha was sitting at her desk on her phone, but she threw it down once she saw me. I laughed and shook my head. She was so scared of me. After I finished walking through the building, I took the stairs to leave. As I got closer to the bottom, I overheard somebody talking.

"Why the fuck are you here?" the guy asked.

"So I can prove to him that this is his son and get my

money," the lady said.

"You supposed to be low-key with shit, and you're all at my job? Go home, now, Ciara!"

"Ok, damn! I'm getting a paternity test done, too."

I could not believe this shit; that bitch was trying to play me. By the time I was all the way at the bottom of the stairs, they were gone. I could not wait to get to the bottom of this.

CHAPTER THIRTEEN

Tara

When Kane and I were dating, he was everything to me. We met four years ago, on my 20th birthday. He was 23 at the time. I didn't celebrate birthdays much. I was just never into them. I was at the gas station filling up my car when he noticed me. I was wearing black sweats with a white tank top and white flip flops. My hair was in a messy ponytail under my black hat. Kane walked over and introduced himself and gave me his number. I gave him a call the same day because I was a loner and need somebody to vent to. I had no family here in Atlanta, so Kane was like an angel in disguise. Once we got to know each other more, I fell in love with him.

He cooked, cleaned, paid all the bills, gave me everything that I ever asked for. All I had to do was be there when he needed me. Of course, I cooked and cleaned for my man sometimes, but he did most of the chores most of the time.

The only thing that our relationship had been missing was him. He was always at work, and he would come home all times of night. I became lonely. I never suspected him of cheating on me. Kane was the man of my dreams. It was my selfishness that drove me into the temptation. Any woman would love a man like Kane.

While I was at the mall one day, I ran into Lea in the food court while I was eating my lunch. We lived in Atlanta, so I was at the Southlake Mall. My fitted skirt and crop top hugged my body. My caramel-colored skin made me look like I was biracial or like I had a tan. I kept my natural hair cut short. I loved wearing long, wavy, Brazilian weaves. My stylist was always sure to fix me up just right.

I didn't think that Lea was checking me out, until I noticed the lust in her eyes.

"Hey," she said as she sat next to me.

"Hey."

Her face was beautiful. She was slim-thick and had a gorgeous smile. I had never really been into girls, so things between us started with a small conversation. She said that we should hang out sometime and then gave me her number.

Sure enough, we began hanging out and getting to know one another. She made me feel special. She was showing me all the attention that Kane was not. But Lea's attention was not always good attention, though. Lea made me leave Kane for her, which I felt bad about doing, and then she started to become abusive. I quickly learned that the grass is not always greener on the other side. Lea had split personalities; she would snap within the blink of an eye.

I had become sick and miserable. Then I found out that I was pregnant. I wanted to tell Kane so bad, but Lea threatened to kill me and my baby if I did. I was scared for my life. Lea tortured me. She barely allowed me to go to my doctor's appointments while I was pregnant, and then she made me deliver her at home. I never understood why she treated me the way that she did. Sometimes, I believed that it was my karma for leaving Kane.

One day, Lea came home and asked me if I wanted to move to Savannah. Of course, I did not want to move. I wanted my man and for my family to be together. However, without a care in the world about what I wanted, Lea sent me to live with her sister and her husband while she stayed in Atlanta. She told me that if I ever thought about going to Kane about anything, she would kill me.

After two years of putting up with Lea, I was fed up. I wanted my family. I wanted Kane, Madison, and me to be together, as one, the way we should have always been. I was going to put Lea's shenanigans on blast once and for all. She was making me give Kane custody of my daughter so that she could continue running my life, but I was determined to put an end to the madness.

I called Kane and told him to meet at the diner that was down the street from the place that I was renting while in Atlanta. It was temporarily though. He agreed because I told him that we needed to talk about Madison. When I arrived, he was already there. He had looked just as good as he did the first day I saw him. I fell in love all over again. I could feel myself getting moist. It had been two years since we had sex, but I was still turned on by the thought of him. Lea made sure that I was satisfied with sex toys and oral sex, but those activities were nothing like having a real man. I'm not going to lie, Lea had that weak in the knees, toes curling, body shaking type of sex. She had my body doing things I never even thought it could do.

"What's up?" Kane greeted me.

He sat across from me at a small table. "We need to talk."

"Talk."

"I'm gonna get straight to the point," I said. "Lea is a fraud. She only wants your money. Two years ago, I met her at Southlake Mall. It was supposed to just be a friendly conversation, but one thing led to another and I caught feelings."

"So you expect me to believe that my girl is a fraud?"

"Kane, I am telling you the truth," I whined.

"And how do I know that you are not lying?"

"I can keep going along with her plan to make it seem like I'm still down, but in the end, I want my family – you, me and Madison."

He rubbed his face. "This is too much, Tara. You can't expect for me to just drop things and run to your rescue."

I grabbed his hand. "Kane, I'm the only woman you need. Me, you and Madison can be a family. I love you so much. I hate that I ran into her that day at the mall."

"What do you want me to do? What do you want from me?"

"Whatever it takes to get back close to you, Kane."

"How I know you ain't lying?"

"Kane, look at me."

I looked into his eyes the way that I did when we were dating. There wasn't a doubt in my mind that he didn't believe me.

"Let me think about it," he asked.

I closed my eyes and shed a few tears, "Kane please. I will do whatever you want me to do. I just want my family back. Lea took that from me. I am sorry that you were not there for Madison's birth, but I promise to keep her in your life. Please don't take my baby from me. Going to court will make me look unfit and I am not. I have no family here. You know that. You and Madison are all I know."

He knew that both my mom and dad were dead. They passed away when I was 8 after our house caught on fire. I was getting off the bus from school when everybody, including myself, noticed the house burning. I broke down to my knees right there and burst out in tears. It was a very sad day for me. After their funeral, I was passed from one foster home to another. Once I turned 16, I was adopted by this lady name Teresa Bandcock. Two years later, she passed away from a stroke. I was 18 by then, and I was on my own from that point on.

Kane placed his hand on my shoulder, "Tara, stop crying. We can figure this out together. I will keep a close eye on Lea. If what you are saying is true, then everything will come to light."

"Thank you for hearing me out, Kane," I cried more. "I want my family. If you take Madison from me, I will lose my mind."

"I will keep in touch."

"Thank you."

"Don't thank me yet," he said before he stood up to leave.

CHAPTER FOURTEEN

Lea

"You need to sit your pregnant ass down somewhere!" I yelled at Ciara. I was in her condo after Q told me that she went to his job.

"Y'all taking too long," she whined.

"Bitch, shut the fuck up. We got this."

Little did anybody know that Ciara was my sister. She and Q had been married for nearly a year, but they had known each other for what seemed like forever. He was always hanging out at my mother's house helping to repair whatever went wrong. Ciara was sent to Atlanta to get money from King, but our mother, Cynthia who we call "CJ," got sick, so Ciara had to move back to Savannah to care for her. Our mom was not diagnosed with anything. She just stayed sick from all the drugs that she was using.

This was what we did – lie, scheme and plot. Laylani didn't know this side of me. To her, I was just a wild girl with a good heart.

There Ciara was, pregnant with Q's baby, trying to frame King for money. Sometimes, it just seemed the bitch's head just wasn't screwed on tight. She had gone a little too far showing up at the office.

"I had to make it seem real," Ciara explained. "I mean, how am I gonna explain to him that it's his son with no paternity test?"

"I got that taken care of," I said. "He'll be paying you child support once every month. Once the fake paternity test comes back, you'll be getting $6,000 a month from him."

"What if he takes me to court?"

"Men don't think like that. He'll be paying you out of guilt because he would want to be in his son's life."

"How would Lani feel with her being your best friend and all?"

"What she don't know won't hurt her."

I wrapped up my conversation with Ciara and let her know to just relax and let Q and I handle things. I didn't want my nephew in harm's way.

I called Tara and let her know that I was on my way over to talk. She told me that she had a plan, and I was eager to hear it.

I pulled up to her house, stepped out of my car and

walked towards the door. It was unlocked, so I invited myself in.

Tara was sitting in the living room watching TV. All she was wearing was her bra and panties. I walked over to her, sat down and gave her a kiss on the cheek. She smiled at me.

"So, what's the plan?" I asked.

"Wouldn't you think it'll make sense to put Kane on child support instead of giving him custody of Madison? If I put him on child support, we'll get money from him every month."

"Makes sense, but I thought you didn't want Madison."

"I never said that. You did."

"Well, when are you going forward with the plan?"

"I've already gone to the child support office."

"Good," I said rubbing my hands together. I had always heard that money could make you cum, and it was making me cum for sure then.

"I gotta go. I need to make these fake paternity test results for Ciara and King. Then I gotta come up with a way to show that he's on child support for her."

"Ok, baby," she said with her eyes glued to the TV.

I knew that what I was doing would eventually come back around and bite me in the ass, but until then, I was going to enjoy every moment.

I headed to my old college friend's house. My old friend made fake birth certificates, diplomas, DNA test result papers, IDs, basically any official paper that anybody needed.

Once I got there, the guard at the door told me to head to the back. I told my friend what I wanted, and he got it done. I paid him and went on about my business.

CHAPTER FIFTEEN

Laylani

Ever since I had found out that I was pregnant, King had been on my ass. All he wanted me to do was stay at home in bed all day. He even moved me into his place so that he could keep a closer eye on me.

The grand opening of my shop had been postponed because King had insisted that I waited until the baby arrived to have it. I was loving the way he pampered me, but my ass was sore from laying around all day.

I was five months pregnant and more miserable than ever, but somehow, I found joy in the fact that I was having a baby girl. Lea was somehow always busy, so I had no one to talk to half of the time. I do not know why she had become so busy all of a sudden, so I decided to go visit her. I knew that King would be upset, but I didn't care. I was tired of lying in bed all day.

When I got to Kane's place, his car was in the driveway,

so I knew he would see me and tell King. I exhaled and walked up to the door anyway. I knocked, and a female who wasn't Lea came to the door.

"Can I help you?" she asked.

"Where's Lea or Kane?" I asked.

"Lea is not here. Kane is in the shower."

"Who are you?" I asked with an obvious attitude.

"I'm Tara, Kane's baby's mom. Who are you?"

"I'm Lani. Can I come in?"

Kane walked out from the back as I walked into the living room. "What's up, Lani?" he said.

"What's going on here?" I asked.

Kane sat down in his recliner. Tara stood next to him. I gave her a look that let her know to not let my belly fool her. She smirked while looking at me.

"Your friend is a fraud," Kane explained calmly. "She's been after our money for about two years now."

"Ours?"

"Me and King. She's so money hungry that she'll do anything to get what she wants. Did you know that Ciara was her sister?"

"Lea doesn't have a sister."

"That shows you how much you know about your best friend," Kane said.

"Why is she after you and King?"

Tara spoke up. "Two years ago, I met her at the mall," she said. "We were supposed to be just girls, you know, just to hang out with. We became lovers and she threatened me to leave Kane for her."

"Hold up," I stopped her. "My girl may be a lot of things, but she damn sure ain't gay."

"Like Kane said," Tara said, "that shows how much you know about your best friend."

"So, what? What are you saying?" I was confused and mad.

"Lea forced me to move to Savannah after she found out Kane had big money. She moved me with Ciara and Q. I was held hostage. Not long after, I found out that I was pregnant with Madison. She didn't allow me to go to any doctor's appointments, and she made me have my baby at home with a midwife, no medicine or nothing."

I was shocked. I had nothing to say. I was so speechless. I thought to myself, *"No wonder she kept going to Savannah. Her mom has been dead for years, so she say. I was wondering why she kept going down there. I even asked, and she told me she needed some closure. This bitch was trifling."*

"You see?" Kane asked.

I just nodded. I was just in disbelief. I knew that I had to get to the bottom of this. People always told me that I could know someone for years and still not *really* know them. I guess I never knew who I could trust.

I left Kane's place and headed home to start dinner. I decided to cook my man's favorites: fried chicken thighs, homemade macaroni and cheese, rolls, and a pound cake for dessert. I was a country girl until the death of me. My mom taught me well. Once King was home, he came straight to the kitchen, hugged me from behind, and kissed me.

"Why are you out of bed?" he asked as he turned me around.

"My doctor didn't put me on bed rest; you did," I reminded him with a kiss.

"I am your doctor."

I laughed. "How was your day?" I asked him.

He exhaled and sat at the table. I sat his plate and his Corona in front of him, and then I went and sat across from him.

"Ciara had the baby, and it's mine," he said as he ran his hand over his face.

"When did you do a DNA test?" I bit down into my chicken.

"A lady came to my office a few weeks ago and took my blood sample."

"Who was she?" I asked.

"I can't remember. She had a mask over her mouth and said she worked with the state paternity office."

I dropped my fork. "Really, King?"

"What, baby?"

"Where are the results?"

He pulled out some papers and handed them to me. I looked over the results, and he was indeed the father of the baby. I was just about to about to agree with him and try to figure out where we would go from there, until I looked a little closer at the paper. "Oh hell no! This shit is fake!" I yelled.

King looked at me like I was stupid. "How?"

I handed him the paper.

I continued, "It says, 'Child support suggests that you pay $6,000 a month.' You have to go to court for a child support order. Have you gotten a letter from the court or even the child support office?"

He shook his head no.

"Is this all you have?"

"Yeah."

"I can't believe this bitch!" I shouted as I paced the room. "Kane told me all about Lea. I'm starting to believe him now. Did you know Ciara was her sister?"

He shook his head no, again.

"This bitch got some nerve," I said. "My mom knows a lawyer. We are getting to the bottom of this."

I was so pissed at the woman that was *supposed* to be my best friend. How could someone be so greedy and desperate for money? I was going to find out just exactly what was going on.

CHAPTER SIXTEEN

Kane

At first, I had thought that Tara was playing, but I quickly realized that everything she said was coming to light. When Tara came into the picture again, Lea wasn't around nearly as much as she had been before; she came and went as she pleased. I wasn't mad, though. I was glad that Tara was around more often, even if it was just because we were trying to make Lea think that we were really going along with her plan. I was really considering killing that bitch, but I decided to wait it out. Lea was going to get what was coming to her one day. Even though Tara left me and I am still trying to get the story right in my head, she was still the mother of my child. I will always love her.

Tara was laid across my couch, scrolling through her social media apps on her phone. I admired her beauty. I had missed everything about that woman. She was my everything, and I was glad that we were getting back to a good place with one another. Even though I'm fighting for custody of my daughter, she's still around. Tara was my first love, so I thanked God every day for letting us share our first seed together.

Tara looked at me and smiled. "Why are you staring at me?" she asked. We had been spending more time together and old feelings started to come back.

"I just really miss you, girl," I told her. "I'm thanking God every day for bringing you back into my life. I was becoming a ho."

She laughed, "I never wanted to leave."

"I know," I said. "You are who I always wanted to be with."

I stood up and walked towards her. I lifted her chin up and kissed her passionately. I knew that she missed this beast because I damn sure missed her blessing down below. Tara had the best sex in town, no lie.

Tara did not resist my kiss. She unbuckled my belt and released the beast that God had blessed me with. My manhood was rock-hard, waiting on her to do her thing. She covered the whole thing with her mouth; she didn't even gag.

"Damn, girl. I missed this shit." I said as I leaned my head back. She kept sucking and slurping. She had me weak in the knees. I was about to bust until she pulled it out of her mouth. "What the fuck, Tara?"

She smiled at me, "I just miss this. I wanna take in the moment. I never wanna leave again."

She put her mouth back on my dick and sucked me until I busted in her mouth. She swallowed my insides and licked her lips, letting me know she liked the way my cum tasted. That only turned me on more. I pushed her back onto the couch and spread her legs wide open. She had already removed her clothes, so I was staring at her pretty, pink pearl. I had noticed that she had gotten it pierced, which was sexier than a motherfucker.

I dove in with my face and licked and sucked on her clit like it was my last meal. She always tasted so sweet. I had never had pussy that tasted like hers before. Her cream saturated my fingers as I moved them in and out of her wet opening.

"Oh, Kane!" she moaned.

Her body jerked and shook. She grabbed my head, begging me to stop, but I couldn't. I missed the taste of her.

"I'm about to cum!" she moaned loudly.

After she came, for what I remember, the fifth time, I stopped. "Damn, boy!" She tried to get up, but I held her down. I eased my dick into her wet soaked pussy. It was tight.

"Kane, it's been so long," she whispered into my ear. "I been dreaming of this day."

I pounded in and out of her as our moans filled the house. Tara was throbbing and creamy. I flipped her ass over and sexed her from the back.

"This pussy so fucking good!" I moaned.

My toes curled, and my eyes rolled to the back of my head.

"I'm gonna nut all in this pussy, girl," I said to her.

"Ahhh!" She moaned as I slapped her ass. "I can't take no more, Kane. I'm cumming, baby. I'm cumming!"

"Me, too!"

I squeezed her ass cheeks and let all my seeds out in her pussy.

"Damn, I missed this shit," I said as I pulled out and spread her ass cheeks. I licked her from behind. Oh, I wasn't done. I flicked my tongue up and down from her ass to her pussy. Tara tried to run from me, but I was holding onto her ass cheeks.

"Kane, please!" She plead. "Ahhh! Ahhh! Baby!"

I stood up. I was rock hard. Tara turned over and pushed me onto the couch. She climbed on top of me and rode me like I was a horse. Her facial expressions indicated that she had missed my sex just as much as I had missed hers. As she was bouncing on my dick, she squirted and creamed all over me.

"Kane! I'm cumming, I'm cumming!" she yelled with her head pointed to the ceiling. I could feel her pussy lips throbbing on my dick, gripping it tight.

I grabbed her ass cheeks and smashed in and out of her.

"Oh shit!" I said as I came inside of her.

She collapsed onto my chest. We were both breathing heavily.

"I love you, Tara," I whispered as I kissed her forehead. "I really do. I have missed you so much."

"I've missed you, too." She lifted her head up and removed her sweaty hair from her face. "I've always loved you, and I always will."

"I want you to be the only woman in my life again. This time, let us take things slow until this mess dies down. We can start over as friends for right now," I said.

"I am down for whatever, Kane."

We kissed and fell asleep on the couch. It was a good thing Madison wasn't there.

CHAPTER SEVENTEEN

King

Months had gone by since Ciara tried to pull that stunt on me. Lani's mom introduced us to a lawyer so we could get to the bottom of this. I was so tired of all the drama that Lea had caused that I decided to plan a nice baby shower for Lani. I knew she had been miserable sitting in the house all day and night, so I figured it would be a nice gesture.

I had Sasha plan everything for me. She hired the best decorator and caterer in town. She insisted that the theme should have been 'Ladybug Layla' since we had decided to name our baby girl "Layla" after Laylani.

The day of the shower arrived, and I couldn't wait to see the look on Laylani's face when she saw all that I had done for her. I invited her aunt, her mom, and her cousins to share the moment. I even invited Lea, but it was up to her to show up.

Before heading home to tell Lani to get ready, I stopped by the maternity store to grab her nice dress to wear. Since the theme's color was red, I chose a long red dress. I also stopped by Kay's Jewelry to grab a ring. I was thinking about taking things to the next level with Laylani. She'd been right by my side through all the drama. She never even asked me for anything in return. I really loved her.

After I left the mall, I headed home. Laylani had no idea what was in store for her that day. I walked into the bedroom with her gifts in my hands. Laylani was laying on the bed watching the Lifetime channel. She could watch that mess all damn day.

"Get that bitch!" She yelled at the TV.

I shook my head and smiled. I put the bags on the bed.

"Here, get dressed," I told her.

"Where we going?" she asked with her eyes still on the TV screen.

"Don't ask no questions," I said. "Get dressed. Your hair, nail, and make-up appointments are already booked. You should be done and ready by 3:00. It's ten a.m. now. Get ready."

Laylani eased her way off the bed. She looked so beautiful pregnant. Her skin was silky and had a special glow to it. My baby was gorgeous. She waddled her way to the bathroom and showered. Laylani was ready within thirty minutes. Since she had hair and makeup appointments, she just showered and threw on some casual clothes.

I drove her around to her appointments, and we were done around the time I had intended for us to be. The shower was at 4:00, so we had time to go home and change. Laylani had asked me why we had done all of that a million times, but I didn't answer. I told her to just be patient.

Once we were ready, we headed to the Hampton Inn in Atlanta for the shower. When we arrived, Laylani's eyes lit up. There was a sign and balloons outside letting us know that the baby shower was there and where to go. I could see tears build up in her eyes. She held onto her baby bump and smiled.

We walked in and everyone was there. Sasha had the place looking good. We ate, played games, opened gifts, and took pictures at the photo booth. Once we were done opening gifts, I figured that it was time to propose.

Laylani spoke first.

"I just wanna thank everybody who took their time to come here, and thanks for all the gifts and the love. Special thanks to my boo, Kingston, for getting all this together for me. I couldn't be more thankful. I love you so much."

I got down on one knee and grabbed her hand.

"Ever since the first day I saw you, I knew in my heart that one day you'd be my wife. The love I have for you is unexplainable."

Tears fell from her eyes.

"Laylani, will you marry me?" I asked.

"Yes, Kingston, I would love to."

I slid the ring onto her finger, and we kissed passionately. I was really about to marry the love of my life. I couldn't believe it.

Just when everything was about to be over, Ciara walked in. Lea must've told her ass about the shower.

"King! King!" she yelled as she walked in. "Where you at? Your son needs you." She walked in with her son in her arms. I shook my head in embarrassment.

"Bitch," I said as I walked towards her. "What the fuck are you doing here?"

"What do you mean? You have a son that needs you in his life while you're over here playing daddy to that bitch baby!"

"Get the fuck out of here!"

Before Lani could stand to her feet, Kane grabbed her arm. "Sit down, sis," he said. "You don't need to get involved."

She yanked her arm from him and waddled over towards us. "Bitch, get the fuck out of here," she demanded. "This is my baby shower, and you're bringing this mess here?"

"I don't give a damn if it's your mama house, King will take care of his son one way or another."

Just when things were about to get heated, our lawyer, Eric Jake, walked up with an envelope in his hands. I invited him in case some shit popped off. He handed it over to Ciara. Ciara grabbed it and opened it to read what it said.

"Oh, hell no!" she yelled. "I know this is a lie!"

Lea ran up and snatched the papers from her and read them as well.

"Who the fuck are you?" she asked our lawyer.

Laylani spoke, "He's our lawyer and the little stunt you tried to pull is dead-- over! How could you do this, Lea? I thought we were best friends."

"We are," Lea replied. "But you know how I am, I love money. And I love what I do."

"But you got your own money."

"Shut up, Laylani! Who asked you anything?"

"Don't play with me. If I wasn't pregnant, I'd beat your ass!"

"Bitch please!"

Before I could grab Laylani's arm, she headed towards Lea. She was stopped in her tracks, though, when a clear-like liquid came pouring down her legs. She looked over at me, holding her stomach, which let me know her water had broken. I rushed over to her and picked her up into my arms.

"Kane, load the gifts in your car. We gotta go."

I rushed my baby to the nearest hospital. She was in so much pain. I had to hurry before she lost her mind. She was sweating, hollering, and cussing at me because she could feel Layla's head coming down.

When we got to the hospital, they rushed her to a room. I held her hand the entire time.

Hours later, our daughter, Layla Marie Wallace, was born. She was healthy and so beautiful. I couldn't wait to get her home and spoil her. Her room was already filled with everything pink. Since Laylani had moved in, I turned my guest room into the baby's room.

When I walked into the hospital room, Laylani was sound asleep. Her mom was spoiling the baby already. I laughed and shook my head.

"Good morning," I said to her.

As I walked over to grab the baby, Laylani woke up.

"Hey, baby," she smiled.

"Why are you awake? You need to be resting," her mom said.

"I been resting for two days. Y'all won't even let me hold

my baby for long."

"Girl, you got the rest of your life with Layla," her mom said.

She just shook her head and smiled, "When am I going home?"

"The doctor said today, so get dressed."

When we got home, we settled in, and I rocked Layla to sleep and then laid her in her bed. Still tired from labor, Laylani was sound asleep, too. I called Kane to see what he was up to.

"Yo?" he answered. "How's my niece doing?"

"She's good. What's going on?"

"You ain't gon' believe this shit, bruh."

"What's good?"

"That nigga Q robbed our asses. Now they all M.I.A."

I stood to my feet. "What the fuck you mean he robbed us?" I asked. "And who is 'they all'?"

"I just got off the phone with Sasha, and she said when she got there this morning, all the safes where opened and the place looked a mess. She called the police, and they are investigating. I ain't putting shit past Lea and them."

"That bitch! Where you at now?"

"About to pull up and get you so we can head over there."

"Iight, bet!"

I went upstairs to get dressed to head out. Lea had lost her ever-loving mind. I had something for her ass, though. Good thing we only keep a certain amount of money in the building because that bitch was about to cause war.

CHAPTER EIGHTEEN

Lea

My whole plan had begun to backfire on me. I had everything planned out the way that I had intended, but things just did not go right. I sent Ciara to get the money from King at first, but then Ma relapsed on drugs again. Then I came into the picture, but Tara's presence messed that up. She was supposed to be laying low in Savannah with Q and Ciara, but somehow, she got away from them one day while they were asleep. Ciara was supposed to keep an eye out. I just knew that once Kane saw Tara that his whole mindset would change, especially once she ran her mouth like a running faucet. I had not been back to Kane's place yet; I figured he was happy that I was gone. Sending Q to work for them had been my next option. He would always be around their money, so it would be easy for him to take it.

I knew everybody was over at the hospital with Laylani

and the baby, so I figured that would be the perfect time to activate my last plan. Ciara, Q, and I were all dressed in black as we headed over to the building. It was dark out, so we knew we could get in without a problem. Q had seen Kane put in the codes a few times, so he knew how to open the safes. We were in and out within thirty minutes. Once we left there, we headed to Savannah.

On the road to Savannah, I counted the money. Q was driving while Ciara and I were counting. The baby was in the backseat with us. After counting it all, we came up with $50,000.

"That's it?" I frowned. "Them niggas broke!"

"You know they're not gonna keep all their money there," Ciara said. "We should have gone to their houses."

"Damn sure should have." I wasn't thinking straight. I had to do something, quick. Robbing the safes *and* their homes was the last thing to cross my mind. "Why you ain't been said that?"

We arrived at my mom's house and ran inside within four hours. She was in the living room smoking a cigarette. She smiled as we walked in with the duffle bags.

"I see the plan went well," she said

"We only got $50,000."

She struggled to stand to her feet. My mom was 52 years

old. She was chocolate just like Ciara and me, and if it was not for the drugs that she was on, she would be just as pretty as we were. Her skin was still somewhat smooth with no wrinkles, but the small craters on her cheeks and dark circles under her eyes made her look older than she was. Her ass hung a little longer than most, but it still had its round, full shape. She was always stressed out, complaining and being negative. The shit got on my nerves at times. "What the fuck you mean?" she asked with a concerned look. "That nigga owes me more!"

"What nigga?" I asked.

"John Wallace," she spatted. "That bitch died on him and he just up and left me. Her insurance policy was supposed to be split between us. He lied and took my money away from me."

"Wait, what money? How do you even know this man? What do you mean, Ma?"

"John, their father, and I had been sleeping around while he was married to my best friend, Susie. She had cancer, and he was miserable with her. He promised me that once she died, we would split the insurance money – $1 million. So when she died, he ran off with his two boys left me."

"Ma, so all of this because of some insurance money that you claim that this man owes you?" I asked her.

"Damn right. He promised me, so I want my money."

"Mom, why didn't you just call the man about your money? If it's *your* money." Ciara had the nerve to ask. "And since you were sleeping with your best friend's husband, is John Lea and I father, too?"

"Or do you even know?" I asked.

Mama slapped the spit out of my mouth.

"I might have been a hoe, but I know who my kid's fathers are."

"Who?" I snapped.

"Bitch, don't be asking me all of these questions."

"So, you don't know, do you?"

"Lea, your dad is this guy that I was messing around with. He was married as well, but he was broke, his name was David. I only fucked him because he was fine. He is dead now. Ciara, your dad and I fucked around once, and you happened. I never seen him after that. I can't even remember his name. It was supposed to have been on some high shit."

"CJ, something is seriously wrong with your trifling ass," Ciara said.

"Oh do not sit here and judge me when you two are doing the same thing."

"We don't do drugs," I said. "And if it wasn't for your trifling ass, we wouldn't be this way. I am out of here."

I grabbed the bags and ran out the door. I hopped in the car and took off. I did not know where I was going, but it was far from there.

CHAPTER NINETEEN

Laylani

Since I had come home from the hospital, I'd been enjoying my baby girl. King had been nothing but great to us. Even after the robbery at the business, he still managed to make sure we were situated. Aside from all of the drama, I was ready to get back to work.

Layla had turned six months, and Lea had still been M.I.A. Even after all she'd done, I really missed her. I'd been calling her and leaving her messages, and I even sent her a few texts to let her know that I had called. I kept hoping that she would respond to me soon.

The time for my grand opening was coming around, and I was excited. Tara and I had become cool since she had been around a lot more, and their daughter, Madison, was the sweetest little girl. Since King and I had become engaged, I decided to combine an engagement party with my grand opening. The name of my boutique was 'Lani Secret'.

My colors for the grand opening were purple, black, and gold.

Right after my grand opening, the party started, which was in the boutique as well. People were snacking on the entrees that the waitresses walked around with and were having drinks as well. I looked around and they all were enjoying themselves. The music was just right. I was all over King as we danced together to the many songs that the DJ was playing. The liquor on his breath let me know that he was feeling the same way as I was.

"Let's go to the back," I whispered in his ear. He smacked and squeezed my ass cheeks, then he kissed me passionately. I almost forgot where we were. I grabbed his hand and led him to the back of the store. We ended up in my office. King closed the door and locked it behind him. I laid back onto the desk and opened my legs. King slid my thong to the side and slid his dick into my wet hole. Because of the short purple dress that I was wearing, it made it easy for King to get to it. All he did was lift it and went right in.

"Ahhh," I softly moaned.

I bit my bottom lip. I loved the way that he felt inside of me. I am glad that I lost my virginity to him. King pounded in and out of me with so much force that my desk was rocking, I thought that it was about to break. I was breathing heavily, and my moans filled the room. It was a good thing the music from outside the door was loud.

"Damn girl!" King moaned out.

I ran my fingers over my clit causing it to squirt. King loved that shit. He fucked me harder until I creamed on his dick.

"Baby, you are making me weak. I'm about to cum!" he moaned.

"Me too baby!" I moaned in pleasure.

"Ahh! Ahh! Ahh!"

We both came at the same time.

We walked to the restroom in that was in my office and cleaned up before we headed back to the party. I knew people were wondering where we were. As we walked out of the office, Tara was at the door with her arms folded, shaking her head.

"Y'all ought to be ashamed of yourselves," she smiled. "Y'all got company."

"Who is it?" I asked.

Instead of her answering me, we all walked to the front where we saw Kane standing. He was standing next to his dad and Lea. I wondered what the hell was going on. Furious at the way Lea repetitively crashed my events, I walked in full speed towards them.

"Before you say anything, let me explain," Lea had the nerve to say.

"Bitch I could kill you right now," King said angrily.

"Son, that won't be necessary," his dad said.

"What's going on?" I asked, confused.

"Can we take this to your office?" John asked. I led them to my office. "Sit down," John said as he directed King and Kane to their seats. "I need to talk to you two."

"Why is this bitch here?" Kane asked. "Can you answer that?"

"Sit down and listen!" John commanded.

They both sat down as directed.

"Now, there's some things that I need to tell you," he said.

I could tell that the issue was serious.

"All of what has happened has been my fault," he continued. "I know it may sound crazy, but I did not know any of this until Lea brought it to my attention a few months ago. Lea's mom, Cynthia Johnson, but she's well- known as CJ; she has been after my money since we left Savannah while the two of you were too small to even remember. It was right after your mom died. Cynthia was addicted to the life that I lived, and I wanted different for y'all. So, I took my wife's insurance policy money, gave CJ some and brought y'all here to Atlanta with me. I opened the business because

I didn't want y'all in these streets like I was. CJ thinks I owe her, but I don't. So, she sent Lea and Ciara here to rob us to get the money that she thinks I owe her."

"Whoa," Kane said.

Lea hung her head low and said, "I didn't know."

For the first time, since I had met Lea, I felt sorry for her. Her mom was so caught up on revenge over something that happened so many years ago.

"You told me that your mom was dead, Lea," I said.

"She was dead to me," she said. "This was supposed to be the last scheme that I pull before I was done with her ass."

"Yeah right," King said.

"I still have the money," Lea said. "After we took it, we went to Savannah to give it to my mom. That's when she told me everything. I was so furious, I grabbed the bags and left. I've been in Decatur since. But I didn't touch a dime of that money. I promise. I'm so sorry. If I had known that my mom was on some revenge for love type of shit, I would have never done this. This was her mess from the jump."

"Lea, this is a lot," I said.

"And it is not her fault," John said. "I am going to get to the bottom of this. I know where to find CJ, so I will head that way and face my own problems."

After the meeting in my office, I wasn't in much of a

mood to party anymore, so I wrapped my event up. Once everyone had left, King and I locked the boutique up and headed home. He was so mad that he didn't speak the whole ride home. He was pissed at his dad for not telling him about the affair that he had with Lea's mom while their mom was dying. John should be ashamed of himself. As soon as we walked through the door, he headed upstairs to take a shower, and then he got straight into bed. It was a good thing I had gotten some already.

The next day, Lea came over, so we could talk. To be honest, I had really missed my friend. She had missed out a lot: the birth of my child *and* six months of her life. And then we also had a wedding to plan!

Lea rang the doorbell, which startled me a little. I had just put Layla to sleep; she had been fussy all day.

"Hey," she said as she walked in and sat on the couch.

"What's up, girl?"

"I'm sorry about the way I've been acting. I was so money hungry. I'm just glad nobody got hurt behind my actions."

"Don't speak too soon," I warned her.

"And I'm sorry again about my mom, but that's what she told us to tell everybody. She was trying to be on the low about the whole 'John' situation, which I knew nothing about at first. Most of her schemes would just be robbing men and women, or even sleeping with them, for money just because. It was never on some revenge for love shit."

"That's just crazy. How could you put your kids up to something so dangerous like this? She's selfish. She could've just told you the truth."

"Right," she said.

"And you never told me that you were into women," I mentioned.

"My bad, sis," she laughed.

"Uh huh," I said. "What's up with you and Tara?"

"That's over with. It was only to get close to Kane. Now he got his woman back."

"What you gon' do?"

"About what? A man? Sis, you know I am good on any man or woman. I gets what I want, when I want."

I laughed, "Just don't keep anymore secrets from me. I missed my friend."

"I got you, I promised," she swore to me. "Where's Layla? I would love to meet her."

I took her upstairs to meet Layla. She was awake again. Lea played and laughed with her. I couldn't help but smile. Lea was my best friend. I didn't care what anybody thought of our friendship. She may have missed out on six months of my baby girl's life, but I had always believed that everybody deserved a second chance.

After I put Layla back to sleep, Lea and I looked up wedding ideas. It was time to start planning my wedding.

CHAPTER TWENTY

Ciara

It had been months since we'd heard from Lea. She had taken the money and left. Leaving Q and I in the dark. He was pissed at not getting his part of the money and so was I. Lea should have let us known something. Quan never knew about my past with how my mom had us sleeping with men and women for money. I lied to him for him to fall for me because I didn't think that he would after he knew about my past.

After Lea and I confronted our mother, calling her all kinds of hoes and bitches, she left. So I got my shit and left, too. I was no longer going to put up with CJ's mess any longer. She had become so money hungry that it was scary. She was so unfit as a mother and she wasn't about to be part of her grandchild's life acting that way.

Lea and I both lost our virginity at a young age because of her. I would have loved to have lost it to somebody that was worth my time, but my mother had other plans. Lea and I were born ten months apart, so everybody always thought that we were twins growing up. We both were born and raised in Savannah, but once Lea got older, around sixteen, she moved to Atlanta with one of the guys that she was sleeping with. He was one of the men that CJ hooked her up with. Of course all of the men were a lot older than us. Old enough to be our dads, but we never asked any questions. Well Lea didn't. I was the one who would cry all the time. I hated that life.

As for Q and I, well, I had bumped into him when I was at the grocery store in Savannah about two years ago. He had been watching me walk up and down the aisles. My long, smooth, chocolate legs were hanging from the booty shorts that I was wearing, and my halter top was showing my navel ring. My hair was in a shoulder-length bob, and I wore heels. They made my ass jiggle.

"Don't I know you? You look familiar," he said. He looked way older than me, but that was nothing that I wasn't used to. I was only 18, he was 43 at the time, but I had been with my fair share of older men.

"I don't think so," I said as I slung my hair.

"Well, I must say you look good," he said as he licked his lips and looked me up and down.

"I know." My mouth had always been smart. Men love that shit, though.

After that day, we kept bumping into each other. He insisted that our consistent, unexpected meetups were fate. We finally exchanged numbers, and from there, we became close. I introduced him to my mom, and I told her that I was in love. After he treated me like the queen that I was, I was very impressed. A little over eight months, he asked me to marry him. But in the mist of all of this, I met King while visiting Lea in Atlanta. That was how we started fucking around. King and I met one day at the bank. We kicked things off from there. He never knew that Lea was mt sister though. While in a fake relationship with him, Q came to visit me while I was in Atlanta. He never knew what was going on, so I acted as if things were normal. King caught me up in my mess, caught me "cheating" and broke things off with me. From that point on, I told Q all about my past . He excepted me and we moved on.

Not long after I moved back to Savannah with my mom, I became pregnant. Of course I knew that the baby was Q, but he and Lea made me throw the fake results in King's face. Even though Lani was Lea's best friend, she was still willing to ruin the man's life. Well at least she didn't sleep with him behind Lea's back like CJ did her best friend.

I had to contact my sister; I needed her more than anything at the moment. The six months that I had spent without her had been hell. We had always been close; she was like my other half. I'd called time after time, and I even left her a few messages. I didn't know what else to do, so I called Lani.

"Hello?" She answered.

"Hey, Lani, I know that I may be the last person that you want to hear from, have you heard from Lea? I haven't seen her in a while."

"You are right about that," I could tell that she had an attitude. I didn't blame her though. I was the girl who was trying to take money from her man. "But yeah, she just left."

I exhaled with a breath of fresh air, "Thank you. Could you tell her that I have been trying to call her? I really need to talk to her."

"I will let her know," she said and hung up. I smoked a few blunts to ease my mind. Josh, my son, was fast asleep. We were in my new condo in Atlanta. I moved here just a few months ago. We were living in and out of hotels until I finally found a place. Within an hour or so, Lea called me back and asked me to meet at Lani's place the next day. I was so happy to hear from her. After talking to her, I took me a shower, bathe my son and hopped in bed.

The next day, I arrived at Lani's place around two in the afternoon. Lea texted and told me what time to be there. When I pulled up, I saw Lea's car and that made me smile. My heart skipped a bit because I was nervous about facing Lani after all that I have done to her and her family. As I approached the door with my son on my hip, I took a few deep breaths. After three knocks, the door slung open.

"Lea, I'm so happy to see you," I said as I damn near jumped in her arms. "Where have you been?"

"I have missed you, too, sis. Come on in," she said as she led me into the living room. When we stepped into the living room, I saw King, Kane, Tara, Laylani, and a man I had never met before. "Sit."

I was still holding onto my son with all my might.

"What's this?" I asked, confused and slightly worried.

"Ciara, this is John Wallace," Lea said. "He is the man that Ma is after."

"Nice to meet you, Ciara," he said as he reached out to grab my hand. "Lea has told me a lot about you."

"Nice to meet you, too."

I was kind of confused as to why he was here.

"I came for Lea," I told him. "I didn't know that everybody would be here. Since everybody's here, I wanna say that I'm..."

"No need to apologize," John interrupted. "Your mom has always been that way. She wants everything to go her way. If not her way, no way. I can say that I'm to blame for that. Before I met her, she didn't want for much. She was her own boss. She got her own money and she didn't need a man for that. She used to tell me that her mom taught her how to get money in a way that no mother should have showed her kid. I guess that is where she get from treating you two that way. She blamed her pass life and lived it through y'all. I introduced her to the game once she met me, and she became addicted to the drugs and alcohol. I'm sorry about everything as well." He turned towards King and Kane. "I should have told you two about this."

"It's all good," Kane said. "You just need to handle CJ before shit get too out of hand."

"I've been trying to reach out to her about all of this," said John. "She hasn't been answering my calls."

"I haven't heard from her since the day we left," I said.

"Well, I'm going down there this weekend. I need to talk to her," John said. "It won't be hard to find her."

"Good luck," Lea said.

"Girl, I am luck," John popped his collar. And we all laughed.

"Can I talk to you for a minute, Lani?" I asked nervously.

She rolled her eyes and stood to her feet, "I guess." I followed her to the back deck of their house, Lea held and played with Josh while I stepped outside. Once we were outside, I lit a cigarette, "What do we need to talk about?

"First off, I am so sorry about what happened. I didn't know that all of this would happen."

She rolled her eyes again, "You're only saying that because you got caught. You knew from the jump that I was Lea's best friend. The same way she knew, you knew. She should have told me what was up from the jump, but whatever. I am so over this. We don't have to be friends and I will not fake kick shit like we are. So you stay away from my man and stay in your own lane, and I will stay in mine."

Well damn. She cut my ass off before I had a chance to explain. Once she said what she said, she went back into the house leaving me there looking stupid. I needed to get out of there and that's exactly what I did. All of CJ's problems were giving me a headache.

After getting myself together, I walked back in and asked Lea to leave with me. She and I needed to catch up on things. I had missed my sister.

CHAPTER TWENTY-ONE

Cynthia

All my life I was a good girl—that is, up until I met John Wallace. I met him when I was 18 working at a local grocery store in my small town in Savannah. He was dating my best friend, Susie, but I didn't know it at the time. He would pick me up from work and then drop me off after we had sex.

He married Susie about eight months after we met. I was shocked and so hurt, but I never said anything because I learned how much my best friend loved him. She had been away at Savannah State University, and apparently John, who was an alumnus, was going to see her every weekend. They planned to marry immediately after she graduated. It seems that everyone knew but me.

Out of guilt, John would still give me money to go "buy nice things," but I felt that he never loved me. When Susie got sick with breast cancer, John needed help with their boys,

King, 4, and Kane, 3. I would go to their house to help as much as I could, and we carried on sexually for a short time before her death. I thought I was the only woman for him, but when it was all said and done, I was the other woman.

His boys were his world, and John thought that I was unfit to continue helping with the kids after her death. He took the boys and moved away to Atlanta, which is why they didn't remember much about me. All they knew was that their mother was sick and had died while they were young.

Once I met Lea's dad, David, I thought things would get better, but they only got worse. He was married. I told him that I was pregnant with Lea, then he left me. He was broke, anyway, but had good looks. He came back shortly after I had her, but he'd only come over at night. Then I met Ciara's dad. Me and a few of my friends were getting high and he was over. It was a one nightstand and I ended up pregnant. After that, I never heard from or even seen him again. I asked my friends if they remember the guy, but no one did. I felt so bad because I was going to be raising two girls that I didn't want. My mom was dead. She had died years ago from a car accident. Here I was depressed and lonely, left alone to raise two kids. I was broken and heartless at that point. To stay numb, I turned to drugs and alcohol. My habit got so bad that I had my girls sleeping with my men for money. I knew it was wrong, but they had to learn like I did. I taught them that pussy was power, and they could and would be taken care of by men if they played it right.

Lea was a pro before Ciara was. I had to beat Ciara's ass a few times because she was a big ass cry baby. All she ever did was ask why she had to do it. Lea was obedient; she did what she was told. I loved that about her. She never nagged about anything nor did she complain. I saw so much of myself in her. As for Ciara, well, I never understood where she got her ways from, probably her father.

Once I came clean to the girls about what I was doing and why, Lea took the money and ran off. I haven't heard from neither one of them since. I was hurt, I felt like I was back at square one, drugs and alcohol. Everyone I have ever loved left me. I know that what I had done to my girls was wrong, but I missed my kids. I needed them more than ever. Six months later, I was depressed and feeling suicidal. They say that karma always come back around, so I figured that I was being punished for treating my girls the way that I did. I knew that one day, I would have to face my problems. Well, that day had come. I ended up in the hospital on a mandatory 1013 hold. For the first 36 hours, I was being held in the psych ward, then I began to get paranoid, demanding to use the phone because I thought someone was trying to kill me in the hospital.

I didn't know how, but John was at the hospital waiting on me to discharge. He was a fine man for his age at 60. He was 6'3" and handsome with light brown eyes and gray, curly, short hair. I fell in love with him back in the day, and I hate how things ended between us. I wanted my family so bad that I would've done anything. John was my first love; he treated me like a queen. I may have been his side piece, but he treated me like a lady. His wife didn't have anything on me.

"What are you doing here?" I finally asked through my sore throat.

"You got some nerve asking me anything. Why the fuck are you trying to rob me, CJ?" The base in his voice was loud.

I sat up in bed and looked him directly in his eyes.

"John, you took everything from me."

"That doesn't give you a reason to rob me. All you ever cared about was money. My boys wouldn't even have mattered in your eyes. You were so money hungry that you sent Lea and Ciara to sleep with them for money that don't even belong to you."

"I earned every dime of that money, John. You promised

me that I would get half of the insurance policy money. You lied to me."

"And I left you with enough money to get your shit together and survive on your own. I didn't want my boys part of that lifestyle, so I left."

I began to cry. "You didn't have to do me like this. I loved you and those boys more than anything, John. That's all I had left of my best friend, and you know that. You took the boys and probably told them I was dead like I was nothing to you. I made sure things were good on my end while you went home and played house. We were supposed to have been a family! It was me who held you down, cooked, clean, fucked you right, made sure home was good while she was sick. You married her and had an insurance policy on her to get the money. Don't sit here acting all innocent like you're an angel when you played a big part in this mess."

"How dare you talk to me like that?"

"Like what? Speaking the truth? What? You can't handle the truth?"

"Shut the fuck up, CJ, before I knock your ass into a coma!" He put his strong hand around my throat.

"I…can't. . .breathe," I uttered as he squeezed my neck. He released his grip and walked towards the window.

"I love you, John." I said with the little breath that I had in me. "I just want my family back."

"You have a hell of a way of showing it."

"I'm sorry, please let me see the boys. I've missed them so much.

"I'll see what they have to say about this," he said. "Get dressed. Let's go."

"Where are we going?" I asked, but I really didn't care as long as it was far away from this place.

"You coming or not?" His attitude was not needed. I did as I was told and got dressed.

We left the hospital and went to John's place in Atlanta. Once we were there, John led me to the bedroom so I could put my things away. His place was so nice. I was nervous because I hadn't seen this man in over 20 years, and yet, there I was standing in his house.

After I showered and threw on some clothes, I walked into the bedroom. John was laying on the bed with nothing but a towel on. My mouth watered at the sight of that man. It had been over twenty years since I'd tasted him. I had to taste him, again.

I got down on my knees and released his beast. John may have been damn sixty, but his penis still looked young and pretty.

I swallowed his penis whole; I made sure that it filled

my throat. I spit on its head and then licked my spit back up. My gag reflex was sharp, so I knew it felt like he was fucking my pussy. I made sure to keep my mouth wet as I pulled him in and out of it. His moans let me know that I still had skills.

"Damn, you've always had the best head in this world," he said as he pushed himself deeper into my mouth.

Once he climaxed, I swallowed every drop and licked my lips when I was done.

"Bend that ass over," he directed me.

"Yes, daddy."

I got on all fours with my face down and my ass up. John went into my pussy slow until he was all the way in. Once he was all in, he fucked me like it was the last time he ever would. After all those years, his sex was still so good. I couldn't believe I betrayed this man; his dick had me wanting to change my life around and marry his ass.

"John!" I yelled out.

He spanked my ass.

"This my pussy!"

"Yes! Always have been!"

"You ain't going nowhere ever again!"

"You left me, baby," I cried and moaned.

He flipped me over and kissed me passionately.

"I'm not going anywhere ever again. I'm sorry."

Those words made me melt. John made love to me for the rest of the night. I fell in love all over again. I was ready to meet the boys and explain why all of this scheming went on. It was time for a change.

CHAPTER TWENTY-TWO

John

I know that it seemed as if I gave in as soon as CJ arrived at my house, but I am a man before anything. Who would turn down the best piece of pussy they ever had? Not me. I am 60 years old and still like to get my rocks off. I have had many women in my days. I have been in only two serious relationships since my boys and I moved to Atlanta. They didn't work out because they were too needy. Not that I did not have the money or time, I was just not ready for a committed relationship. No matter the age, if you are not ready then you are just not ready.

CJ and I met one day while she was working at the local grocery store down in Savannah. I did not know that she and Susie were best friends. Susie and I was in college together, CJ did not go to college. She was already in the streets, but she played the role of a good girl when we met. I took her and introduced her to my street life. Susie was not fit for that life though. She and I made plans to marry and move out of Savannah, but once we got married, she was diagnosed with breast cancer. She had already had King and Kane. They both were three and four when Susie was diagnosed.

CJ would watch my boys for me while I was out doing my dirt in the streets. CJ was my main ho, and she was okay with that. She cooked, clean, sold my product, hid it for me, held my guns, fucked and sucked me right whenever I wanted it. All of this while her best friend/my wife was dying. King and Kane were too young to understand, so I kept it that way. CJ was there for me so much, that I promised to give her half of the insurance policy when Susie dies. I am not going to lie, I was in love with CJ, but once Susie died, I promised to leave that life behind. I even mentioned it to CJ, but that was not what she wanted. That's when she started using my products, getting high off of it.

A few months after Susie died, I packed the boys and our stuff and moved to Atlanta. I left CJ with enough money to get herself together. Nobody told her to spend all of her money on drugs and dick. Once I left Savannah, that's what I did, left Savannah behind. My life there was supposed to be over. I never would have thought that CJ would come after me after all of these years. I guess that's what good dick do to you.

Here we are today, she was sounded asleep in my California King bed after making sweet love to her. CJ still looked good as she did the first time I saw her. A little older, but she was still beautiful. I slapped her on her naked ass causing her to jump out of her sleep. I stood over her fully dressed in some basketball shorts and tank top.

"Get up, CJ," I demanded her. "We need to talk."

She rubbed her eyes and looked toward the clock, "John, it's eight in the morning."

"I know what time it is," I snapped. "Now get up."

She rolled her body over and slid her feet into her slippers that were beside my bed. Right before we went to sleep, she unpacked all of her things from her bags. I walked into the living room with her on my tail. By then, she was covered with her robe.

"What's up?" She asked.

"We need to talk about what's gonna happen now."

"What do you want to happen?" She asked me.

"I have always loved you CJ, but the things that you have done to me and my boys are just greedy and so low."

"I know, John," she said. "I am changed now. Being in that hospital made me think about a lot of things. I prayed that you would come to my rescue, my prayers were answered. I promise that I will not do anything to harm you or your boys. I was stupid and was not thinking. I could have just come to you instead of sending my girls. I was an unfit mom, so setting Ciara and Lea up to do my dirt came easy to me. If you can't trust me at this moment, then I understand. We can work on that part. But John, I love you. I do. You are the only man that I have ever loved this way."

"I hear you," I said. I was sipping on my coffee from my coffee mug. "A lot of things have changed for me. I am retired now. King and Kane are both over my business. And no it is not an illegal business, it's legit. If you want any part in my life from this day forward, you are gonna have to make some changes on your end."

"John," she walked towards me and bend down on her knee to grab my hand. I was sitting in my recliner chair with my feet propped up. "I promise that I will do whatever it takes to get back on your good side. I loved them boys then, and I can get to love them even more. Once I meet them again."

"If you are willing to change, I will set something up for you to meet them," I said. "It may take some time getting used to."

"I know. I know," she said. "Whatever it takes, I am with it."

CHAPTER TWENTY-THREE

King

"Yo," Kane said through the phone.

"What's up? Did dad call you?"

"Yeah, talking about meeting up with CJ?"

"Yeah. What you think about that?"

"I don't know, man. Like what's the point? She owe Pops the apology, not us," Kane said.

"I feel you. I am just going to support my pops," I said.

"I really don't want to, but I guess so," he said.

"Yeah, come so that we can hear them both out. I want to know what she has to say."

"Alright man," he said. "I will see you tomorrow."

After I ended the call with Kane, I headed to Layla's room. She was sound asleep in her playpen. Laylani was at her boutique handling things like a boss; I was proud of my baby. After checking on Layla, I went into my man cave and rolled a blunt. My mind was racing. I didn't know whether to trust my dad or CJ. My mom was dead, so what did I need to meet her for? Since my dad went to Savannah and get her, he has been locked up in that house with her. Ain't no telling what has been going on over there.

My dad hasn't been involved with anyone for as long as I can remember. He have had a few female friends from here and there, but it was never anything serious. He used to always tell Kane and me that his soulmate was dead. I hated to hear that though. Knowing that my mom died while Kane and I were so young.

After I finished smoking my blunt, my phone vibrated; it was Ciara, I ignored the call. Laylani was the only person I could go to about my problems outside of Kane. I mean I loved my pops, but that shit was too much.

Once I was done with my thoughts, I decided to call Ciara back to see what she wanted. She better not had been on some bull shit.

"What's up?" I asked.

"Can we meet up for lunch, so we can talk?"

"For what?"

"So that we can talk," she said.

"We don't have anything to talk about. Your son is not mine, so you do not need to contact me for anything," I said to her.

"Why you gotta be so mean, King?"

I laughed before I knew it, "Don't get all sensitive on me now. Bitch you wasn't sensitive when your ass tried to get me for my money."

"I told you that was all CJ's idea," she fussed.

"Yeah, whatever."

"So, can we meet up and talk?"

"We talking now ain't we?"

"You don't have to have an attitude," she snapped.

"Bitch," I smacked my lips, "Do not contact me anymore. Lose my number." I hung up on her.

I decided to go see my lady. Her birthday was the following weekend, so I wanted to do something special for her.

Once I was at Laylani's boutique, I got out the car and walked in, surprising her with a dozen roses and chocolate. She was occupied with a customer when I walked in, so I nodded my head letting her know to meet me in her office. She smiled and let me know she'd be there once she was done. After about fifteen minutes, she walked into the office and sat across from me.

"Hey, handsome," she said. "Thank you so much." She was referring to the roses and candy.

"You are welcome beautiful. How's everything going?"

"Going good. You okay?"

"I'm okay-- just need to get away. And since your birthday is next weekend, let's get out of here and go celebrate."

"Go where?" she asked, excitedly.

I handed her the tickets that I had in my hands.

"Virgin Islands. The flight is already booked. We leave Monday and come back next Sunday."

"Oh my God! Baby!" She came from behind the desk and hugged me tight. Then, she kissed me passionately.

"I love you so much," she said.

"I love you, too."

"Baby, I can't thank you enough."

"You can thank me by releasing some of this stress I got built up inside of me."

She laughed and dropped down into a squat position. She went in on my dick with her mouth. Not long after, I released all my stress into her mouth. She licked and swallowed every drop.

"I love when you do that shit," I told her.

"I know it." She smiled and went into the restroom of her office to brush her teeth.

"So, what's been going on with John and CJ?" she asked. "Are y'all going to meet her or what?"

"Pops wants us to. I'm still thinking on it."

"I think you should," she said. "I mean, think about it,

she hasn't seen y'all since you and Kane were five and six. I think you should give her a chance."

"But she's not my mama," I said.

"But she was there for you while your mom was going through what she was going through. For all you know, and I am sorry to say this but, she may have been the lady that you remember as your mom. Think about it, baby. All you remember about your mom is her lying in bed all day. CJ was around helping your dad with you and Kane all times of the day. Just give her a chance."

I exhaled. "I'll meet up with my dad and CJ and see what's up. He's having a dinner this Sunday and wants us to come."

"Do you want me there with you?"

"I may need you to hold my hand through this."

"Fine, I'll ask my mom if she can watch Layla for me."

"Okay, baby. I'll see you later at home," I said as I stood up to kiss her. Then, I headed out the door.

"I love you," she said yelled behind me.

"I love you, too baby!"

Sunday had come around before I knew it. I was a little nervous because this would be the first time in over 20 years that I had seen this woman. After we left Savannah when we were young, my dad never said anything else about her or our mom. Kane was a momma's boy, so he would ask questions every now and then, and especially around birthdays and holidays. She would come across my mind every so often, but I was a little more mature than Kane to know that she wasn't coming back. So, I accepted that fact and moved on. While she was laying on her death bed, my dad never let us see her much. The only time we saw her was during doctor's visits and at her funeral. I didn't remember CJ at all.

As I adjusted my shirt in the mirror, so many things crossed my mind. Thank God that Laylani, and a few blunts here and there, was there to ease my mind.

"Baby, are you ready?" Laylani asked me. She was standing at the door wearing some high waist skinny jeans, a red crop, and red pumps. Her red lipstick was popping and made her lips look full and sexy. She had her hair hanging down her back that day; she usually wore it in a bun.

"I'm ready," I said, fixing my jeans.

I was wearing my black Levi jeans, a red fitted puma t-shirt, and my red pumas.

"Let's go," I told Laylani. We walked to the car and headed to my dad's. Once we were there, Laylani grabbed my hand before we stepped out of the car.

"You're gonna be fine."

"Thanks for coming."

We walked towards the door. Once we rang the doorbell, the door swung open and there she was, standing there. My heart skipped beats as I looked at the gorgeous older woman standing in front of me. Her skin looked so smooth and her hair was full and healthy. She had a few gray strands here and there, but she was still beautiful. I began to have flashbacks. All this time I thought that this woman was dead, but she was the woman who was there all along – from my first day of preschool all the way up until my dad took us from her. Seeing her face made things much clearer. I remember the night she sang us to sleep and put a Band-Aid on my cut when I fell down. It was CJ all this time, not my mom, Susie.

So many mixed emotions came upon me, I didn't even realize that I was crying. Before I knew it, I had pulled CJ into a tight hug. I held her like I was a kid all over again. She smelled so good, just like I remember. I could feel Laylani's hand on my back. She was rubbing it up and down trying to calm me down. I couldn't help myself, though.

She pulled from the hug and lifted my head up to her.

"It's okay," she said, comforting me. "I'm here now."

I looked back at Laylani. She was standing there smiling at me. She was always there for me, which made me love her even more. That was the first time she had ever seen me cry. I'd never shown my emotions in front of a woman like this.

CJ led us into the house where everybody else was seated around the dining table.

"It's about time," Kane said and they all laughed. "I'm starving."

"Shut the hell up," I laughed. "I'm here now, let's eat."

CJ cooked everything. It felt like Thanksgiving that day. She cooked dressing, collard greens, fried chicken, macaroni and cheese, ham, turkey, candy yams, custard, red velvet cake, and pound cake. I felt like a kid in the candy store. I had never had a big dinner like this before. Laylani cooked for me, but not like that. I was going to have a heart attack trying to eat all this food. Once everyone was stuffed, we sat around and chatted.

"That was good, CJ," my dad said.

"Yeah, everything was hitting!" Kane said.

The rest of us nodded our heads in agreement.

"Since we're all here," my dad said, "I would like to introduce you guys to someone very special to me. This is CJ," he pointed to her. "Cynthia Johnson. She was your mother's best friend, and she helped raise you when you were young. She became like a mother to you. I fell in love with her…" his words began to trail as Cynthia stared at him in shock. Like she had never felt he truly loved her at all. "Your mother was a good woman. She and I got married, and that's when you two happened." He pointed at Kane and me. "I'm sorry for how all of this has played out. I really lost all contact with CJ because I didn't want the two of you in the streets like I was. I wanted a fresh start, so I took your mother's insurance policy money and put all of my illegal money into a legal business. I left CJ with enough money to survive on her own, but not all that she had asked for. So that's why she came after me all these years later. Once again, I'm so sorry for the hurt that I've caused on this family. I just thought that CJ wasn't fit to raise the two of you and I needed y'all with me."

"Pops, that's all in the past now. Let's live in the moment," Kane said.

"He's right," I said. "Let us enjoy this time now."

I thought that meeting would have leave me so mad at her. I had so many questions, but once I saw her, all of that anger went out the window. My emotions had taken a toll on me. If it wasn't for Laylani, I didn't know how I would've handled the situation.

"Kannon and Kingston, can I talk to the two of you alone?" CJ asked. "Let's step outside."

We followed her outside to the balcony. Once we were outside, CJ lit a cigarette.

"Want one?"

We both shook our heads no.

"Thanks for hearing me out," she said. "I'm not the same person that I was when the two of you were young. I'm willing to make a change if y'all let me be a part of your life."

"You're here now, aren't you?" Kane asked. "Let's just take it one day at a time."

"He's right. Let's just take things slow."

"Thanks for giving me a chance. I won't let you down."

We hugged and headed back into the house. Ciara, Lea, Tara, and Laylani were all sitting in the living room talking and laughing.

"Lani, let's go," I said as I looked at them. "My head is killing me, and I need to lay down."

"Okay, let me grab our to-go plates from the kitchen and I'll be right out. Do you need me to drive?"

"Yeah."

Once Laylani had the food, we headed home. I took something for my headache and went to sleep. I slept for the rest of that day. When I finally did wake up, it was three in the morning. Laylani was sound asleep next to me. Her arms were wrapped around my neck. I smiled at her beauty. I rolled over to go use the bathroom, and once I was done, I laid back down next to Laylani. Before I closed my eyes, I grabbed my phone. I had a few missed calls and text messages from Ciara. Without looking at the messages or returning her calls, I put my phone back down and rolled over to go back to sleep.

The following morning, Laylani was up cooking breakfast when I opened my eyes. I got up to wash my face and brush my teeth, and then I headed downstairs. I walked into the kitchen to see my baby fully dressed ready to go.

"Good morning, baby," Laylani said to me as she sat my breakfast in front of me on the table.

"Good morning, beautiful. I see you're ready."

"I am, and I'm up waiting on you. I heard you up in the middle of the night. I figured you were tired. The flight leaves in an hour, so eat up."

I laughed and ate my food then we were headed over to the airport. I was about to get away from this mess and help my baby enjoy her birthday.

CHAPTER TWENTY-FOUR

Laylani

It was my birthday week and King and I were off to celebrate. I wanted Lea there so bad, because she was my girl, but I'd enjoy her company once I was back. Once we were at the airport, we had to check in, get searched, and all that other mess before we could take off. Right before we boarded the plane Kane walked in with Tara.

"Oh my God! I didn't know y'all were coming!" I exclaimed.

"You know my bro wasn't going to no island without me," Kane laughed.

"Hey, girl! Let's celebrate!! I'm so excited," Tara said as she grabbed my hands.

"Baby, I want the window seat," I said to King.

"Anything you want."

I smiled and kissed him. I was so excited. We both sat down and held hands the entire flight. It was my first time flying, so I was scared. But with my king next to me, I knew that I was going to be okay.

Three and a half hours later, we were at our destination. The sight was so beautiful-- the water, the rooms, the bars, the whole view. Once we were settled in our rooms, we all headed out for something to eat.

"Baby, I love this," I said as I kissed all over King.

He couldn't help but smile.

"It's beautiful, just like you," he said.

"Aw, thank you baby."

"Can y'all two wait until y'all get back to the room?" Kane and Tara said, laughing.

"Shut the hell up," King and I laughed.

We ordered our food and drinks and enjoyed our evening. The whole time we were out, I felt like somebody was following us. I didn't want to say anything to King because he would've said I was tripping. Once we were done eating, we headed back to our room. We all decided to chill in the rooms that night. Kane and Tara came over and we played games and took shots. I was trying to enjoy my birthday, because I hadn't had any fun with all the drama that'd been going on.

"Y'all two suck," I said to King and Kane. Tara and I were whipping their asses in spades.

"Y'all let some girls whoop y'all asses," I said jokingly.

"Y'all got lucky," King said.

We all laughed.

After about six shots of Hennessy, King and Kane were drunk. Tara and I decided to head downstairs to the bar for a few more drinks.

"I'm having fun. This is nice," Tara said.

"Me too, girl." We sat at the bar and ordered drinks.

"I got to go pee, are you okay to sit here by yourself or you are going with me?"

"I'm okay, I will stay right here." She said. I walked away.

When I came out the restroom, Tara was up dancing to the music over the speakers. I joined her and danced my ass off. I wanted to clear my mind of all that has happened over the past few months. There has been so much going on that I just wanted to enjoy my day like it was my last. I hate that King was too tired to join me tonight, but I know that my man has a good time in store for me as the week continues. For long, I lost count of my shots and drinks. And so did Tara. She was feeling herself so good, she fell onto the floor.

"Girl, are you okay?" I asked her while lifting her up from the floor.

"Yeah, let's get out of here. I'm ready for bed."

I laughed, "Yeah bitch, let's go."

Once we got to the room, I helped King into the bed, and then I climbed in myself. I knew that my first day there would be tiring because of the flight. I figured it was okay to rest on the first day since we were going to be there all week anyway. Besides, it was three in the morning.

Later that morning, King was cooking breakfast. I could smell the bacon in the air. Yes, my man did it all. Once I was out the bed, I freshened up and headed into the kitchen area. My man was standing there with nothing on but his boxer briefs on; they fitted his ass just right. When he turned around, I couldn't help but notice his manhood's print. I wanted it so bad, I was becoming moist.

"*This* is for later," King said as he grabbed his penis. "*This* is for now," he said as he pointed to the food.

I licked my lips and smiled. "Whatever, it's my birthday. I can have whatever I want when I want it." I walked towards him and grabbed a hand full of his beast.

"Later," he smiled as he placed the food on the table.

"Why you gotta do me like that? You got the beast showing through the briefs and won't give me none."

"The same way you up in here with your bra and boy shorts on. Gotta a nigga hard as a rock."

"You ain't right," I laughed.

My baby had cooked eggs, sausage, bacon, and pancakes.

We also had orange juice, which he poured into some wine glasses. We ate and chatted; I was loving it.

"What's on the agenda for today?" I asked him.

"Why you asking all these questions?" King asked with a smile.

"Fine." I said as I threw my hand up. I knew he was up to no good.

Once we were done eating, we showered and put on our clothes. King told me to dress comfortably, so I decided to wear my high-waisted jean shorts, a crop top, and sandals. He didn't want me wearing heels that day.

"Hurry up, baby, Kane and Tara are waiting on us," King yelled from the door.

I was finishing up my makeup. When I was done, we headed to the beach.

"Why you didn't tell me to grab my swimsuit?" I asked.

"It's a store right next to the beach."

"Tara, come with me," I said as I yanked her arm.

I went into the store to grab a two piece bathing suit. Once I paid for it and we left the store, I went into the restroom at the beach and changed my outfit. King and Kane were already settled in a spot by time Tara and I came back. They had already fired the grill up, so Tara and I sipped on our margaritas under the umbrella.

"Wanna go jet skiing?" King asked Kane

"We are, once we eat."

While they cooked, Tara and I chatted.

"So, what's been going on?" I asked.

"Nothing-- just taking care of Madison while Kane works all the time."

"How old are you?"

"I'm twenty-four," she said.

"Do you have licenses in anything? Like do you ever think about becoming a boss bitch? I can't sit around and let a man take care of me."

"I'm fine with spending his money. He doesn't mind."

"Yeah, bitch, but I can't do that. I'm not about to sit on my ass all day taking care of no baby. I love Layla true enough, but I'd be damned if I sit on my ass all day watching her. I can sit on my ass in my office and get paid," I said as I sipped my drink.

"I'm okay," she said.

This bitch was spooking me out. I had to keep an eye on her ass.

After we ate, we all headed to the jet skis. I had so much fun with my king. The water was so beautiful.

After jet skiing and shopping around, we headed back to the room. King was acting as if he was in a rush. Once we were at the door of the room, he looked me in my eyes and kissed me passionately. I was so moist. I wanted him right then and there.

But, he stopped in the middle of the kiss and said, "Lani, I love you so much. You came into my life and changed me. I want to spend the rest of my life with you. I want to have a house full of kids running around getting on my nerves and turning our hair gray," he laughed. "Let me show you that you're all I need."

King opened the room door and my eyes lit up. The room was filled with balloons and rose petals and candles. Each balloon had a picture of us on the end of the string. Next to each candle was a flashcard of the things he loved about me. My heart melted. The farther I walked into the room, the more tears of joy I cried. On the bed, were roses laid to form a heart, and there were also more balloons hanging from the ceiling. In the middle of the heart of roses was a big Michael Kors bag that had been opened and filled with jewelry, shoes, outfits, a small handbag, and a smaller Michael Kors purse.

"Come this way," he said as he led me to the bathroom. The jacuzzi tub was filled with bubbles and warm water.

"How did you do this and I was with you all day?"

"I have my ways of doing things," he smiled. "Now drop

them drawls and hop in this tub." I did as I was told and got naked and into the tub. King came back into the bathroom with two glasses of champagne in his hands. He was now naked, and his beast was slanging from side to side. I couldn't help it; I became moist. "Take this, I wanna make a toast to us," he said. "For the rest of our lives."

"Forever and always."

After downing the champagne, King washed my body. He then climbed in with me and pulled me close to his warm body. He was facing me. He pulled me in close enough to where I could feel his beast poking my pearl. He kissed my neck and licked my nipples. They were now standing at attention. I just couldn't help myself. King was the best at what he did. My pussy was tight every time he entered it. He slid his beast inside of my warmth and motioned himself in and out of me, slowly. My moans filled the bathroom.

"King, you feel so good to me." I told him.

"I know."

"You know just how to make me cum."

"I know."

He was being cocky, but I loved that shit.

He then lifted both our bodies up in the air and eased in and out of my wet pussy as he stood up in the tub. I was holding on to him for dear life. My hair was dripping wet and so were our bodies.

"Ahh!" I moaned.

King had his strong arms wrapped around my body, holding me tight. He then lifted my legs over his shoulder and pounded in and out of me. I had to hold on to the rail in the tub.

"King, baby! I can't take no more!"

He knew that when I said that, I only wanted him to go harder. I was holding onto the rails, grinding on his penis.

"Shit," he moaned. "Girl, you better stop before I bust inside of you."

"Do it."

"Ahhh shit!"

I grinded faster, because I was about to cum myself. I creamed and squirted all over him. He pulled out right before he nutted and dove his face inside my wetness. That man had me so weak. He held my hips as I grinded on his face. Once I had nutted for a third time, he carried me to the bed. He placed the new bag on the floor and laid me across the roses. Once he licked my body down, he flipped me over on all fours and licked my asshole. I swear I was about to take off running. It felt so good to me. King tongue kissed my ass so good. He went from my ass to my vagina and then back to my ass, again. He was holding my hips, so

I wouldn't move. My baby was putting it on me. I knew that the next day, I would be tired.

"King, please. Ahhh! I. . .can't. . .take. . .no more!" I squirted so hard; I'd never squirted like that before. King put his beast inside me from the back and pulled me close to him. He eased all of himself inside of me, inch by inch. I felt him getting bigger after each pump.

"Damn girl," he said. "This pussy is damn good."

"I love you, King. I love you so much."

He smacked my ass, "Oh, you do?"

"Yes, this your pussy. Fuck me! Fuck me, baby!"

"I love you girl. I know this my pussy. It fit my dick like a glove!"

"I'm cumming, King, I'm cumming."

"Ahh shit!" he moaned. "Fuck!"

We collapsed on the bed, breathing heavily and sweating.

"I know you don't think that I'm done," he said in between breaths. "You're getting this dick all night."

"King, please let me have a break."

"Break my ass. This is for your birthday."

"Well I don't want a birthday for another three years," I said. We both laughed. He kissed the back of my neck and I could feel his nature rising. He flipped me over and slid himself in from the front. He had my legs pinned up over his left shoulder pumping in and out of my "wet wet".

"Oooo wee," I moaned. "Why you doing this to me?"

"I love you, Lani. You're going to be my wife one day."

Those words made me melt. I just laid there and let my man have his way with me. He wouldn't let me ride him, he didn't want me to throw it back, nor did he want me grinding. He wanted me to just lay there and take all of him in. I felt like I was in Heaven. King put it on me so good, I was in a zone; the king zone. God knew he blessed that man with size and talent. I thought that if I wasn't so new to that treatment, I probably wouldn't have been so sore. King was a beast with a beast. He had my mind so gone. If he ever would have decided to leave me, I would be so heartbroken. I wanted this night to last forever.

We made love until the following morning. I was too weak to move, so King brought me breakfast in bed.

"You've done enough," I smiled while sipping my orange juice. "I can barely move, and we stopped making love a few hours ago."

"It's your birthday," he said. "It wouldn't be right without birthday sex."

"That sex was enough to last me until my next birthday," I laughed.

"Yeah, right. You want this dick now. I can hear it in your voice."

"Whatever," I fanned him off. "Thank you, for all of this. I love it and I love you."

"Anything you want, I can get it. I love you too."

He kissed me, and I finished eating. That was by far the best birthday ever.

CHAPTER TWENTY-FIVE

Tara

Since Kane and I reconnected, everything had been going great. He and Madison were getting along just fine. She loved her daddy, and I loved him, too.

Once Lea confessed all her wrongdoings, there was no need to go along with our plan. Of course, I wasn't going to put Kane on child support. Why would I have, if we were going to be together, forever? I loved that man with everything in me.

Once we were done with the jet skiing, Kane and I headed back to the room. Our room was right across the hall from King's and Laylani's. Kane and I decided to shower and head over to the bar since King had something nice set up for her birthday. He had hired a designer to set their room up for her. He sent pictures of the finished product to Kane's phone, and it looked good. I thought it was so nice of him to do that.

"What are you drinking, baby?" Kane asked me. I was daydreaming when he asked. "Baby," he snapped his fingers at me.

I came back to reality. "I'm sorry, baby. I'm just a little drained from the jet skis."

"Do you want to go lay down after a few drinks?"

"That's fine with me."

"Okay, cool. Bartender, can I get two Coronas and one shot of Hennessy?"

The guy nodded his head and gave Kane what he asked for.

"And for my girl, she wants a house Margarita."

The guy fixed our drinks and handed them over to us. Kane downed his beer and shot, as we vibe to the music. I was only supposed to have a couple of drinks, but I ended up having five. I was tore up. Kane carried me to the room, and I woke up naked the next morning. I smiled at the sight of my body and Kane's naked body. He was sound asleep, snoring and all. I had a few flashes from our drunk sex from last night. Kane had put it on me so good.

I climbed out of the bed and took shower. I could hear Kane coming into the bathroom.

"Good morning," I yelled over the running water.

"Good morning," he said. "You tapped out on me last night."

"Boy stop," I laughed.

He laughed, "I'm about to cook breakfast. Anything in particular that you want?"

"Whatever you cook, baby."

"Okay, I'll see you in a bit."

He washed his hands and his face and brushed his teeth. Once he was done, he headed into the kitchen. I finished my shower, threw on my robe and headed into the kitchen. Kane was flipping pancakes like he was born to do it. I smiled, walked up behind him and kissed his neck.

"Don't start something you can't finish," he said.

"Oh, I always finish what I start," I teased.

After he was done cooking, he placed the plates on the table. We ate and then got our day started.

Laylani wanted to go out on the yacht and chill. Anything was fine with me, as long as I was away from that man. We all wore white to the yacht. Laylani had on a white one-piece swimsuit that was opened on one side, revealing the side of her stomach. I had on a two-piece bikini, and the guys had on white linen suits. The view of the water and sky was beautiful.

Laylani and I laid across the front of the yacht, sipping from our glasses. The ride was smooth; I thought I was going to get sea sick, but I didn't.

Nighttime came around, and the yacht party began. It was crowded and hot, but we were enjoying ourselves. Laylani didn't let up on King; she danced on him all night.

The party ended a little after midnight. We headed to our rooms and drank a little more.

"It's my birthday bitch!" Laylani yelled as if I wasn't standing right in front of her.

"Happy birthday, girl!" I screamed.

"Let's play some games," she suggested.

"What do you wanna play?" King asked, smoking a blunt with Kane.

I knew what I wanted to play. I mean, Laylani was looking damn good. And since I had already had my first lesbian experience with Lea, I'd been dying to try some things out with Laylani, even though she always made it clear that she had never been into women. The way she's feeling that night, though, I knew that I may have been able to get lucky; that's *if* King would let me.

"Let's play 'never have I ever'," I suggested.

"Never have I ever played that before," Laylani laughed.

"It's like if I say something and you have done it before, you take a shot. If you haven't, you get a pass."

"Let's play."

"Never have I ever kissed a girl," I started.

Everyone, except Laylani took shots.

"Never have I ever received a dance from a stripper," Laylani said.

We all took shots.

"Never have I ever told a lie," King said.

We all took shots.

"Let's play truth or dare," Kane said. "And I dare you two to kiss."

"I'm not into girls," Laylani said.

"That's not what your mouth says," I said.

"No, that's what my mouth, body, *and* soul say."

This was going to be hard, I thought. Kane knew what he was doing. I've told him plenty of times how good Laylani looks to me.

"It's only a kiss," Kane said.

She looked over at King. "You're okay with this?" she asked.

"That's up to you."

She looked at me and stood to her feet. "Just one kiss."

I smiled as she walked over to me. I got into the position to kiss her. Her lips were so soft, just as I had imagined. The liquor on her breath let me know that she was most definitely feeling herself. I slid my tongue in her mouth and she accepted it. I thought maybe she would resist, but she looked as if she enjoyed it. As I grabbed her head, she pulled away from our kiss.

"That's enough," she said as she walked back to her seat. I know she enjoyed it; I could tell by the way she sat there with her legs crossed. One day, I would have my chance. One day.

"Can we go?" Laylani asked King. "I'm getting sleepy."

"I'm ready when you are," King said.

"I'm exhausted from the yacht anyway," she said.

They got up to leave. King and Kane dapped each other up, and then they left. I knew what was wrong with Laylani. That kiss had made her horny, and not for King. Once they were gone, Kane and I headed to bed.

CHAPTER TWENTY-SIX

King

The rest of the time we spent in the Virgin Islands was full of relaxation. After showing my baby the best birthday she'd ever had, we headed back home. She had really enjoyed herself; I could tell by the way she was sexing me. She was showing her appreciation by putting it on me. I damn sure enjoyed her.

Once we were home, we stopped by her mom's place to get Layla. I had really missed my baby girl. I couldn't wait to hug on her. We'd been gone a week, so I knew she missed Mommy and Daddy.

We walked into the house, and I could hear crying sounds coming from the living room. We walked in, and Lea, CJ, and John were standing around while Laylani's mother, Nellie, was crying while her dad, Danny, was trying to console her.

"What's going on? Where's Layla?" Laylani asked. "Mom, what happened?"

"Baby, calm down. Come sit next to me," her mother said.

"Where's my baby?" Lani asked. "And why are you crying?"

I grabbed Laylani by her arm and guided her over to the couch. "Baby, let's sit down and see what's going on."

Nellie started talking. "She's not here," she cried.

"What do you mean, she's not here?" I jumped up.

"We have been calling the two of you nonstop," Danny said. He was tall, big, and caramel skin complexion with a patch of curly black hair that sat on his head, "We have contacted the police and they are on it."

"Wait," Lani started to cry, "What happened, Mom? Who has my baby?"

Kane and Tara ran through the door.

"What happened? I came as soon as you called," Kane said to my dad.

"You know my gas pump is on the opposite side of the car," Nellie said. "She was on the other side in her car seat. I was on the phone and once I was done, I saw a man try to get in the driver's seat. My door was unlocked, so he was able to open the door and grab Layla. My first instance was to run after him, but he was too fast for me to catch him. I hollered and screamed for anybody to hear me. A few men at the store tried to help, but he was long gone by then. He hopped in his truck and took off with my poor grandbaby."

"Mom!" Lani cried. "My baby!"

"She did all that she could," Danny spoke.

"When did this happen?" I asked.

"Today, a few hours ago. He took my purse, too. I had just left the bank. He took my money and Layla. The clerk at the store called the cops. They ran the tape, but the guy had his face covered."

"Who could do this?" I yelled as I jumped to my feet.

"Son, calm down," my pops said as he grabbed my arm. I yanked away from him. "King, we will get to the bottom of this. I will make a few calls around town and see if anybody has seen or heard anything."

"Did you see what kind of truck he was driving?" I asked Nellie.

"A black Silverado," she said. "The windows were tinted and there was a driver, but I could not see their faces."

"Could you tell if it was a woman or a man that was driving?" John asked.

"No," she cried. "I am so sorry, Lani. I promise that I am."

"Mom, it is not your fault," Lani cried and hugged her mom. "It could have happened to me."

"She's right," I said. "Let's all just calm down. We will get through this. Pops, let's go. So that we can go look for some answers. Kane, you riding?"

"Damn right," he said. "That's my niece."

"Baby," I grabbed Lani's face. "I will find out who has our daughter."

She sniffed and wiped her tears, "Okay, baby. I love you so much. Please bring my baby home."

"I got you. I love you, too."

After we kissed, Kane, Pops and I left to see what the streets were saying. My dad was known around town from his business, so people respected him. Plus, he was an old school pimp back in the day. He was well known. We were going to get to the bottom of this rather the police were involved or not. I was going to find out where my baby girl was. Even if somebody was going to answer me in blood.

CHAPTER TWENTY-SEVEN

Ciara

I felt so bad to even be a part of that mess with Q. He was so desperate to get the money that we stole from King them, that he was willing to kidnap Layla. I did not want to go along with the scheme, but he told me that if I did not go through with it, he would kill me. Since we left Savannah a few months ago, Q has been abusive. He beats me whenever he wants to. He started doing drugs not too long after I had my son. It was bad. So bad that he did both the drugs and beating me in front of Josh.

I heard the doorbell and knew it was him. I unlocked the door and before I could open it, he pushed his way inside. He grabbed me by my neck and said, "What took you so long to open the door? Were you in here talking to somebody?"

"No! I promise," I cried.

He loosened his grip. "I'll kill you if you're lying to me," he said.

"Q, I've never lied to you. Please, don't hit me."

"Yeah, whatever," he fanned me off. "Shut that crying baby up!" barked Q and pushed me toward my son.

I walked towards Josh to pick him up. "I was in the middle of feeding him," I told him.

"Fuck that shit!" he yelled. Then he slapped me. "Now shut it up, the both of you!"

I rubbed the side of my face because it stung. I asked, "What are we going to do about Layla? She's been crying all day and asking for her daddy."

"Where she at?"

"I just put her to sleep," I said. "I gave her something that will help her sleep."

"Good because I am not in the mood to hear no damn crying," he said. "Now, how much did she take from the bank?" He was referring to Lani's mom. We had been following her all week. She was making deposits and withdrawing money at the same time every day. I caught on to her routine, that is how we ended up robbing her.

"Only $5,000," I said.

"Damn, that's it?"

"Yes, that's it."

"Have you talked to Lea?"

Lea doesn't even know that I am behind all of this, "No, not yet. Do I need to call her?"

"No, fuck her," he snapped. This was not the guy I fell in love with.

After talking to Q, I laid Josh down for bed. It was late and I was exhausted. Layla was locked in the room at the end of the hall. I had a camera that was connected to my phone so that I could see her from anywhere in the house. Once I laid Josh down, I took a shower and headed to bed. Q was gone by the time I was done with my shower. I didn't know the full story behind all of this, but I knew that it eventually would come out.

CHAPTER TWENTY-EIGHT

Kane

All of this drama was really opening my eyes. I felt as if I could not take any more drama. Whoever dumb ass kidnapped Layla, they better count their days. King has not slept since. Here it is, day three and the police have not found anything yet. It was like Layla had disappeared off the face of the earth. I felt so sorry for my bro, so bad that it had me second-guessing this whole situation with Tara.

Yeah, we have become a lot closer over the past months, but I felt myself moving too fast. I felt like all of this was a rush to me. I mean, she did leave me for Lea's trifling ass, and I still do not understand why she is still alive. After all of the things she has done, she still got to walk around here like everything is okay. The only reason that I am cool with everything is because of my dad. He wanted us to drop the beef since it was basically his fault, but my guard was still up.

Tara was the love of my life. When I love, I love hard. And she took advantage of that. All she had to do was stay home and be my housewife. Of course she was not my wife yet, but it was coming. A little more patience and it was coming. After being around her for this long, I felt as if things was not going to work out as I thought it was. I was second guessing this whole relationship.

"Are you sure that this is what you want?" My lawyer asked. I was sitting at his desk, across from him, getting ready to sign some paperwork. I was filing for full custody of Madison. I want my daughter with me in case Tara would be on some more bullshit. I needed to have my ducks in order just in case some more shit popped off.

"I am very sure," I said as I grabbed the pen from the table.

"How is she going to feel about this?"

"I really don't give a fuck," I said. "Excuse my language, Greg, but I deserve to have my rights when it comes to Madison. I don't want Tara to get in her little moods again and think that it is okay to just get up and leave. This time, my daughter won't have to be involved in her flip flops."

"I understand," Greg said.

"Just thinking about what I went through when she left

me. How broken I was. I do not want to go through that heartache again."

Greg nodded his head.

"I can only imagine her getting in her little feelings and taking Madison away from me. So before she gets the idea in her head, I want to have my rights on paper."

"Totally understand," he said. "Sign here, and here. She will be served as soon as tomorrow. I am going to take this over to the sheriff's office once I leave here."

"Thank you, man."

"That is what I am here for."

My dad has been telling King and I to get a lawyer for years. We have been hardheaded and not listen. Since King almost got scammed by Ciara, he has most definitely taken it more seriously, and so has I. I just could not let Tara take my daughter away from me. I put a stop to it before it can have a chance to happen.

The next day, Tara was blowing my phone up. She was at her place. We hadn't moved in together yet. Shit was moving a bit too fast. I had to slow down and catch myself. I was falling back in love with the woman who betrayed me. After letting the phone go to voicemail on purpose for about 10 times, I decided to answer.

"Yo," I said into the phone. I was sitting at my desk in my office.

"Why the fuck would you file for full custody of my daughter like…"

I cut her off, "She's my daughter, too."

"You know what I mean," she yelled. "Why would you do this to me, Kane?"

"I have my rights. I am her father."

"I know that, baby," she began to cry. "And I would never take that from you, Kane. You know that."

"I don't know shit. For all I know, you can get Madison and leave my ass. Then I will never see her again."

She exhaled, "Kane, I would never do that."

"Well, it's too late. I am filing for custody. I will see you in court."

"What about us?" She cried. "I thought that what we had was something special again."

"We need to slow down, Tara. I can't let you do that to me again."

"I won't. I promise."

"Whatever," I snapped. "I will see you in court."

"Kane, please." I hung up. My mind was all over the place. I kind of felt bad. Only because I have a soft spot for Tara. It has always been that way. With her coming back into my life, I have grown to love her again. I just need to pump the brakes a little. After talking to her, I decided to hit King up and see what the update on Layla was.

"What's up, bro?" He answered.

"How's it going? Have you heard anything?"

"Pops was supposed to get back with me an hour ago, but I haven't heard anything. He was supposed to call Elroy and see if they have heard or seen anything," he said.

"Keep me posted," I said. "Have you been to sleep?"

"You know that I will," he said. "What's sleep? It's been two days and I don't have a clue where my daughter is. Lani is worried sick about both me and Layla. She's not been eating or sleeping as much either. It's rough man."

"I am sorry, bro. This makes me want to do what I am doing even more now. I am filing for full custody of Madison. I need her with me at all times man."

"You got to do what you got to do, bro," he said.

"I love you, man. If I hear something on my end, I will let you know."

"Alright, bro. I love you, too."

CHAPTER TWENTY-NINE

Lea

It had been almost a week since we last saw Layla. Lani was sick from her disappearance. I had to be there for my girl because I loved Layla as well and Lani was my best friend. Our bond had begun to get back to normal after all the drama that had went down. I could tell that she still had her guard up, but I couldn't blame her. I even respected the fact that she didn't want Ciara around her at all. With her and King having a past, I just dealt with the two of the when the other one wasn't around.

I had been trying to contact Ciara since Layla had been missing. She has been ignoring my calls and texts and I did not understand why. She was so anxious to get in touch with me and all of a sudden, the bitch is gone. After trying to the umpteenth time, I decided to pull up on her. Her condo was not far from where I lived, so I arrived in no time. Once there, I hopped out my car and headed up. Once I reached the door, I heard arguing between her and Q.

"Bitch I will kill you," Q yelled. Then I heard a scream and cry from Ciara's mouth.

"Please stop hitting me, Quan," Ciara begged. "You are upsetting Layla and Josh."

Layla? Did this bitch just say what I thought she said? I banged on the door. While banging on the door, I sent King a text letting him know where I was and that Layla was inside.

"Open the damn door, Ciara!" I banged on the door.

Q yelled, "We busy!"

"Q, if you hurt my sister, I will kill you with my bare hands. Try me."

The door unlocked from the inside, I pushed my way in. The place was a mess. The lamps on the tables were knocked over. The TV was busted, the couch was flipped over, and clothes were everywhere. Ciara was laying on the floor with Layla and Josh in her arms while crying. I ran over towards her to help her up. I grabbed the kids from her arms. I was so focused on Ciara that I didn't even notice Q standing over me with a gun in his hands.

"You are going to have to use that on me," I said with an attitude. "Because if you don't you will regret that you didn't."

"Bitch, get the fuck out!" Q yelled at me.

"If I leave, Ciara and the kids are leaving with me."

"Ciara ain't going nowhere!" He pushed the gun against my head.

"Look, I don't want any problems," I said. "Just let me take my sister and we can go. Nobody has to know what happened here. I will say that we found Layla in some park or something."

"Why should I trust you?"

"Q, you know me," I smiled trying to throw him off. Josh and Layla was crying to the top of their lungs. "You know that I ain't no snitch."

He started rubbing the gun again his temple and mumbling something under his breath. As he turned around, I pulled my phone out letting King know the condo room number. I was not about to die today. By the time he turned around, I put my hands in the air.

"Shut those crying mother fuckers up!" He yelled.

I grabbed Josh and Layla and took them in the other room and closed the door. I knew that things were about to get ugly because King said that he, Kane, and John were downstairs. I started to get nervous. I gave Layla a snack and Josh his bottle and headed back in the living room to where Ciara was. Her face was so beat up, she had blood everywhere.

"I am going to get you out of here, sister," I whispered to Ciara. "King them are on their way up."

Soon after, Q had calmed down and took a seat in his recliner chair. He was getting high off cocaine. Ciara was out of it. Q had beat her damn near to death. Her eyes were closed shut and her lips and nose were busted. A few moments later, a bang was at the door. It caused Q to jump in fear. He grabbed his gun and ran towards the door. I prayed at that very moment that God would get me and my sister out of there safely.

Before asking who was at the door, King kicked in the door. I grabbed Ciara and hid behind the nearest couch. I heard gun shots after gun shots. I know that those babies were so scared. I couldn't help but wonder what was going through their minds. I closed my eyes and cried, praying for all of this to be over with. Once the gun shots stopped, I peeked my head over the couch.

The scene before me brought tears to my eyes.

CHAPTER THIRTY

Laylani

Getting that phone call from Lea made my heart drop. She called me with both good news and bad news. My heart stopped when she told me that there had been a shootout with King, John, Kane and Q, and that she found Layla. I didn't know if I was to be happy or sad. Running through the hospital doors with tears streaming down my face and my parents right behind me, I ran to the nearest desk.

"I am here for Layla, King and John Wallace," I said impatiently to the lady at the front desk.

She lowered her glasses and looked at me, "And you are?"

"King's wife," I said, while breathing hard.

"I.D. please."

I rolled my eyes, "Lady, please."

"Lani!" Lea yelled and caught my attention. "Over here."

I ran full speed towards Lea with a tight hug, "Lea, where

is King and Layla? Please tell me that they are okay." I cried so hard that I fell to my knees. I felt strong hands on my shoulders. I assumed that they were my dad's hand, so I never looked up. I just kept my head down praying to God that he didn't take my man and my daughter away from me. "God, please don't take my babies away from me. Please!"

"Mommy!" I heard my baby yelled my name. I looked up and it was King's hands on my shoulders. I grabbed his legs and hugged them so tight. He put Layla down and I grabbed her in a bear hug. King wrapped his arms around both of us while we all stood in the middle of the floor hugging and crying.

"Mommy has missed you so much, baby." I kissed all over Layla's face. "I love you, Layla. I love you and Daddy so, so much."

King kissed me, "And we love Mommy so, so much."

"Where's John?" I asked.

"He is back in surgery," Kane said. "He was shot in the hip, but he's going to be just fine."

"Of course, he is," CJ said. I was so caught up in my family moment that I didn't even notice anyone else there. CJ, Lea, my parents, King and Kane all sat in the waiting room waiting for the doctor to let us know what was going on. By that time, John had been in surgery for two hours. Lea had been back and forth checking on Ciara, who was beat very bad. She pulled me to the side and explain everything that had happened. King's bullet shot Q in the left arm and another one in the chest, killing him instantly. Q's bullet hit John in the hip, which is why he is back in surgery. I am just glad that all of this mess is over with. King told me about Kane and Tara, so I was expecting her not to be here.

Soon after, the doctor came from the back, "Family of John Wallace?" We all stood to our feet. "He is okay," he said.

"Thank God," Kane said.

"A little sore, but he will be just fine."

"Thank you so much, doc," King said.

"Yes, thank you so much," CJ said.

"No problem, it is my job to do what I do," he said.

"We really appreciate it," King said.

"He is asleep right now, visitors are allowed in a few hours," the doctor said. He walked off and we all sat around until visiting hours. John's best friend, Elroy, and his wife, Victoria, was there as well. They arrived a few moments after the doctor came out. I held onto Layla and King the whole time. I was so happy that my baby girl and my husband was okay. John, too, for that matter. All of this mess can go to rest now that Q is dead. But there was something about CJ that I couldn't put my hand on. I was just going to leave the thoughts in my mind. Maybe I was wrong.

After waiting around for a few hours, the family was allowed to go to the back. John was sitting up watching TV. His eyes lit up once he saw us all walk into the room.

"Pops," King said, "how you feeling?"

"Better than I was a few hours ago," John replied.

"Luckily the bullet didn't paralyze you since it hit a nerve."

"Nothing can get me down."

"Well, I am glad that everything's okay," CJ said while holding John's hand. "Thank you, Jesus."

"How is Ciara?" John asked. "Is she okay?"

"Yes, she is doing just fine," CJ said. "She is a little bruised, but she will be just fine." Lea had Josh in her arms while I held on tight to Layla. "Thank you, guys, for handling him and ending this feud. All of this was on me, but I am a changed woman now."

"He had my daughter," King said. "And he robbed my mother in law, what did you expect?"

"You're right," CJ said. "Thanks again."

I squeezed King's hand, "I am hungry. I haven't eaten in days."

"Me too," he said. "Let's go eat."

Kane yelled behind us, "I'm coming, too."

“I’m going down to Ciara’s room and sit with her,” Lea said. “See you guys later.”

“Later,” King said.

CHAPTER THIRTY-ONE

Kane

I had a lot on my mind, especially the fact that Pops was in the hospital and I was in court trying to get custody of Madison. It was not that I didn't love Tara, I do, but I just needed to be careful this go around. My pops taught me well when it came down to the ladies. I figured if he can forgive CJ, then I could forgive Tara.

After leaving the hospital, King, Lani and I went to grab something to eat. My bro was so happy that his family was back together. I can only imagine my life without my Madison. Since Tara brought her into my life, our bond is unexplainable. I love that little girl so much I know that I will kill for her.

My pops was released from the hospital within a week. He was on bedrest for three weeks, so CJ would take care of him. We all took turns going over to look after him, though.

He was getting better day by day.

Here we were, the day of court. Tara had been quiet since she received the papers. We haven't been spending as much time with each other at all except during times we had to trade off Madison. I wanted her to know that it was all love, but I just wanted to be more cautious in case she tried another one of her stunts on me again.

I walked in the courthouse with my attorney. He or someone in his law firm had always been able to work magic with their cases, and I was praying he could do it today.

We all had to wait outside the courtroom before being called in by the bailiff. I saw Tara talking to someone who I assume was her lawyer, but I didn't care. King came with me for moral support and to remind me of anything I may have forgotten when telling the judge how trifling Tara is.

When approaching the judge, I was first. The judge spoke first, "Kane Wallace, how do you appear to be a fit parent for this child?"

"Well, your honor, I have a job. I am the co-owner of Wallace Construction Company. My dad recently retired and passed down the business to my brother, King, and I," I pointed at King. "I have a place to live for Madison, and it is in great condition. She has her own room and play area, a big back yard where she can run and play safely." I handed the pictures of my home, inside and out, to my lawyer so that he could hand them to the judge. "I will hire a nanny if I need to, and Madison will be attending school not too far from my home once she turns four."

"And when will she turn four?" She asked.

"August 28th."

She looked over the pictures that my lawyer gave her. She lowered her glasses and looked towards Tara, "And you? What do you have to show proof that you are a fit parent for Madison?"

"I am her mother, for God's sake," Tara cried. "Never have I ever showed Kane any signs of me being an unfit parent to my daughter,"

"You left me and had her with no doctor present and kept her away from me for two years," I yelled.

"Order!" The judge hits the gravel.

"I am sorry your honor," I plead.

"Continue, Ms. Anderson," she said, referring to Tara.

"Okay, that is true, but you know what happened. I was taken away from you forcefully. It was not in my power to leave you. Kane, you know that I love you. I always have and always will. But if you take my daughter from me, it will be devastating. You know that I don't have any family. Please, can we just agree on joint custody? I will lose my mind if you take Madison away from me. When I was going through what I was going through, Madison gave me the strength to keep pushing. I prayed to God every night to guide my way back to you, Kane. I promise that I did not mean any harm. I am not an unfit parent. I love Madison just as much as you do. I will never take her away from you, intentionally. If I could take it back, I would love to experience my baby's birth with you. Kane, please don't take Madison away from me," Tara started crying. My heart became weak for her. Her beautiful face was filled with tears and I could not help myself, but to feel bad for her.

"I'm sorry, Tara. I didn't know that it was that hard for you," I said from my seat.

"It was hard then and you are making it even harder now," she said while rubbing her stomach.

"What? Are you pregnant with my seed right now?"

She nodded her head, yes. "I am 12 weeks pregnant. I didn't know how to tell you. Once I came up with a way of telling you, I got the papers in mail about court and you wanting custody of Madison."

I tried to walk over, but Greg stopped me in my tracks, "What are you doing?"

"I can't take Madison from her," I said to him.

"Are you sure about this?" He asked me.

"Positive," I said as I turned my attention to the judge. "Your honor, I don't want to go through with this anymore. I am sorry to have wasted your time."

She said what she said and dismissed the case. Once we were all outside, I ran into Tara and Madison. Madison ran into my arms and I picked her up planting kisses all over her face. Tara walked over to King and me with a smile on her face.

"I was going to tell you," she said.

"It's okay," I said to her. "We will get through this together."

"Kane, we are having twins."

"Twins?"

"Yes, I found out yesterday," she said while handing me the ultrasound. "I will never leave you again. If you give me a chance to prove myself. You'll see that I am serious about us."

I looked at King, and he shrugged his shoulders, "Bro, it is up to you. Can't nobody make you trust them. It is your choice. I am behind you with whatever decision you make. Just be careful."

"Thanks, Bro," I said. "I will."

Trusting Tara was not even the big issue; it was trusting the motherfuckers on the outside. Before all of this happened, Tara was my everything. Her leaving me turned me back into a hoe, something that I never wanted to be. Now that she is back, I can work on myself, focus on my little family and live life. I can't just take Madison from Tara like I thought that I could. Once seeing her in court crying and all, my heart melted for her.

"Daddy, can we go get some ice cream?" Madison asked.

"You can have whatever you like, baby girl." I kissed her small cheek and we walked off towards my car.

King yelled from behind me, "I will see you later, Bro."

"Later," I said.

CHAPTER THIRTY-TWO

Laylani

After all of the drama that had happened, it was time to plan my dream wedding. King said that I could have my wedding wherever I wanted to have it and that I could have whatever I liked. I chose to have it in the Bahamas. My maid of honor was Lea, and Tara was one of my bridesmaids. Of course, my mom and aunt were there. King's best man was Kane. His groomsmen were Lea's new boyfriend, Stacy, and John's best friend; and his father was there.

Our wedding's theme colors were peach and white. Of course, King wanted to do red and black, but I didn't want to do that for my wedding. He told me to pick out everything, including his tuxedo. He said he was just going to show up. Our honeymoon was going to be in Jamaica, and I was really looking forward to that.

I was ready to spend the rest of my life with the man

of my dreams. Once we said our vows and our 'I do's and kissed passionately, I was proud to be called Mrs. Kingston Wallace. I couldn't wait until our honeymoon; my pussy was throbbing for my man.

Once we were done with the wedding, we headed for Jamaica while everyone else headed home. I needed some long, good loving with no interruptions. I knew that Layla would be safe now that Q was gone, so I wanted to enjoy every bit of my vacation.

I was ready to enjoy my life with my husband. My boutique was going so great. Business was going so good. I was making my own money and not depending on a man for anything. King wouldn't let me spend any of the money I earned, though, because he felt like that's what he was there for. So, instead of spending my money, I put it into an account for Layla to have once she got older.

John and CJ had become a couple, which is all she ever wanted anyway. I was happy for her; she was sober and had been looking like a new woman. She was working for me at my boutique and was doing a damn good job. So far, there hadn't been any drama. I prayed that things would stay that way. Kane and Tara were good again. She was pregnant with twins and the glow on her was so beautiful. I can only imagine being pregnant with two little blessings. Ciara didn't come around anymore, which was okay with me. I didn't want her around anyway, so she kept her distance. She may be Lea's sister, but she did have a thing with my husband. I just don't trust her at all.

I was just happy that everybody was getting along with one another. Life was so much better without the drama. There was so much more to life than messiness and revenge, because when it's all said and done, karma is a bitch.

STAY CONNECTED

Follow me on Instagram and Facebook

Give me feedback on how you feel about my book(s), as I will be coming out with more soon. Stay tuned for "After It's All Said and Done," which is a follow-up or sequel to this book.

www.ingramcontent.com/pod-product-compliance
Ingram Content Group UK Ltd.
Pitfield, Milton Keynes, MK11 3LW, UK
UKHW040006200726
13854UKWH00001B/73

9 781736 848302